Murder at the Statue of Liberty

By Manny Strumpf

PublishAmerica
Baltimore

First printing

At the specific preference of the author, PublishAmerica allowed this work to remain exactly as the author intended, verbatim, without editorial input.

ISBN: 1-4241-1333-4
PUBLISHED BY PUBLISHAMERICA, LLLP
www.publishamerica.com
Baltimore

Printed in the United States of America

Dedicated to my wife Phyllis without whose love, support and encouragement this novel would not be possible, and to the dedicated men and women of the National Park Service whose commitment to protecting and preserving our natural and historic sites and resources has earned them the world's respect.

Acknowledgements

Little did I realize when I became a public affairs officer for the United States Department of Interior's National Park Service in 1978 that the next twenty-two years would become such an important part of my life. I benefited immeasurably from knowing many dedicated men and women, several of whom deserve special recognition.

I am indebted, for example, to Retired Deputy Director Herb Cables Jr. who encouraged me to enter federal service. Kevin Buckley was a highly regarded superintendent of the Statue of Liberty and later, at Gateway National Recreation Area, who also earned my admiration for his professionalism and friendship. I wish you good health, Kevin.

Of my numerous colleagues in Washington, D. C., three in particular stand out. They are Priscilla Baker and George Berklacy, retired Park Service directors of public affairs, and Sandra Alley, former public affairs officer for the Park Service National Capital Region.

I was privileged to have worked with Major Tom Pellinger and his colleagues at the United States Park Police New York Field Office whose insights and confidence made my professional life easier. And how can I not recognize and personally and publicly thank my former secretary and assistant Carole Silano for maintaining order in the New York Public Affairs Office. Carole was always available when called upon and is truly a class act. I wish her and her family all the best.

My editor, Stuart Meyer of Manhattan, helped me refocus this novel and deserves much of the credit if the book is as successful as we both hope it will be.

My wife Phyllis, our daughter Lori and her husband Ron, our son Jeff and his wife Sue, and our grandchildren Scott, Beth and Jennifer, have been and continue to be inspirations and remain the highlights of my life. Thanks, Scotty for designing my Website.

Lastly, I am indebted and grateful to my late parents Ben and Jennie Strumpf, and to my late "Aunt Fannie." These immigrants and children of immigrants encouraged and made it possible for me to enjoy the blessings of the United States of America and inspired me to appreciate the meaningful symbol of the Statue of Liberty. They lived the "American Dream" to the fullest, every day of their lives for which I am eternally grateful.

I relied to a great extent during the writing of this novel on my recollections of working at the Statue of Liberty. The characters are all fictional and are, in part, figments of my imagination, as is the scenario that most likely could not actually have occurred. I take full responsibility for all descriptions and characterizations in this novel.

Manny Strumpf
Spring, 2006

Murder at the Statue of Liberty

CHAPTER 1

National Park Service Ranger Jennifer Marcus stood in the morning shadow of the Statue of Liberty. The magnificent Manhattan skyline was familiar and usually comforting to her, but not today. The handgun in a leather holster hanging from her belt did not lessen her fears.

The young woman's anxiety heightened as she stared at the tall buildings that extended into the cloudless urban summer sky. Several minutes later, she retrieved a metal key from her trousers pocket and reluctantly inserted it into the huge bronze door at the base of the monument. It took extraordinary effort before she was able to slowly pull the door open so that she could squeeze her small body between the door and its metal frame. She made a mental note that the hinges squeaked and needed to be greased. She then pulled the door closed behind her and quickly turned the latch to make certain that the door was securely locked.

The temperature had been in the high nineties and weather forecasters had predicted that the heat wave would extend for several more days. Yet, the coolness and dampness inside the empty darkened structure caused the young park ranger to shiver so she instinctively wrapped her arms around her chest for warmth. When she felt more comfortable, she focused the bright beam of her flashlight against a far wall and carefully walked toward it. Her right hand brushed instinctively against her holster. The eerie silence appeared to be deafening as she reached to open the box that encased the circuit breaker board and as she turned each switch to the *on* position, she was suddenly bathed in soft light.

The young woman continued to grip her flashlight tightly as she cautiously climbed the stairs leading to the second level. An odd but familiar odor suddenly gripped her nostrils. It was a woman's perfume. She felt her heart beating heavily through her gray uniform blouse. She again felt uncomfortable, alone, nervous and frightened. Her hand once more brushed against her holster.

"Oh my God!"

"Oh my God!"

The ranger flushed in shock and panic. On the faded carpet in front of her lay the body of a young woman. The corpse was approximately the same age as she was. Its eyes were open and seemingly focused on the ceiling. It appeared that the woman was in a deep sleep.

"Oh my God!"

"Oh my God," she cried again.

"What am I going to do?" the ranger screamed. She wept as paralysis suddenly and rapidly swept through her quivering body. Her screams grew louder but no one heard her. Her screams suddenly turned to tortured sobs. Her body shook in a cold sweat. Jennifer Marcus desperately tried to regain her composure but her mind went blank. She tried to conceive of a plan of action but she could not think.

Several minutes later, she knelt beside the body and placed her ear to the woman's chest in an attempt to determine a heartbeat, just as she had learned to do at the Academy. She lifted the woman's hand and pressed her fingers tightly against the wrist. She grasped the lifeless form for several more seconds. Satisfied that there was neither a heartbeat nor a pulse, she brushed the hand lightly with her lips and replaced the hand gently on the carpet. She began to sob once again before removing her two-way radio from its plastic case.

My name's Mike Finnegan. I'm a lieutenant with twenty-four years of experience with the United States Park Police. I just described the circumstances that led to the toughest case of my career and I want to give you a full accounting of what actually happened and how we solved the homicide.

I was getting ready for work when the body was discovered. It was a little after seven-thirty and I was shaving.

"Mike. Telephone. It's the dispatcher and he says it's very important." My wife Marge was making breakfast and came running into the bathroom to tell me. I quickly rinsed off the lather, splashed on cold water, walked to the kitchen, and picked up the phone.

"We got a call from the superintendent at Liberty Island," the dispatcher told me. "They found a body inside the monument. I alerted the chief and I think I woke up his wife. He told me to call you. He wants you to lead the investigation."

"Damn it to Hell," I muttered under my breath.

"What was that, Mike?"

"Oh nothin'. I was just talkin' to myself." I grabbed a pad and pencil from a small Lucite rack on the side of the refrigerator and scribbled the name and phone number of the supervisor on duty at Liberty Island. To say I was nervous is a gross understatement.

My grandfather, my father, and my father-in-law weren't happy when I joined the Park Police. They all retired as New York City Police Department inspectors. That's the highest rank you can achieve. They wanted me to follow them into the NYPD, even asking my wife Marge to convince me to change my mind. I wasn't going to be compared to my "old man," my grandfather, and Marge's dad. I realized when the dispatcher called me, therefore, that this case could change my life. It could enhance my career or I'd fall flat on my face. I envisioned my old man telling me that if the NYPD was the lead agency, the case would be solved more quickly. I was determined that it wouldn't end that way.

"Call the supervisors of the Criminal Investigations Branch and

Marine Patrol Unit. Tell them to meet me in the office in an hour. Tell them that I'll brief them when we get there."

Because New York State grants us concurrent jurisdiction and peace officer status, we're able to call in the New York Police to help with major investigations on federal property so I told the dispatcher to also call Detective Sergeant Vince Torre. Torre was a tough New York City cop. We had worked together on other cases.

"Ask him to meet me on Liberty Island. I'll clear docking for their launch." I then called William Johnson, the deputy chief ranger on duty at Liberty Island.

"I was expecting your call," Johnson said when he heard my voice. He had picked up his phone after the first ring. He then briefly summarized what I already knew. I told him to keep the night staff on the island and to close the island to visitors until we got there.

"I already told the staff they're not going anywhere until the police talk to them," Johnson responded. I told Johnson to remain calm, make certain the doors to the monument were secured and that no evidence on the second level was tampered with.

I knew that William Johnson, the experienced National Park Service ranger who graduated with honors from the Federal Law Enforcement Academy, had already taken every precaution possible to secure the facility.

"Already done. The superintendent just called to tell me that the regional office in Boston is aware of it. He's ready to assign the regional law enforcement officer to help you. I said we'd call if we need help. I assumed you don't want regional people hanging around and getting in the way. The ferry company's been told there'll be no ferries going out of New York and Jersey City to Liberty Island today but they can expect service to resume tomorrow."

"Anyone else besides the superintendent and your rangers know what happened?" I asked.

"Not that I'm aware of."

I assured Johnson that he did the right thing.

"One more thing before I forget. I also called Ron Gaines," Johnson added. I muttered several four-letter expletives.

Gaines was the chief ranger and Will Johnson's boss. He was arrogant and derived pleasure from embarrassing his staff in front of others while taking credit for good work they did. My only dealings with him involved law enforcement and security issues. I'd have to figure out how to keep him out of the way, but that would come later.

I replaced the receiver and finished shaving. My wife had breakfast ready by the time I got into my uniform. We ate in relative silence. I got to the office earlier than planned and waited for the arrival of the others. I then gave them a general rundown and we drove to the Park Police dock in Lower Manhattan where we boarded our launch for the fifteen-minute sail to Liberty Island.

Johnson was pacing the wooden planking when we arrived. His head was down and his hands were tightly clenched behind his back. He appeared as if he had been up all night. He forced a weak smile and extended his hand to each officer as we climbed onto the dark brown wooden dock.

"Sergeant Torre said to tell you he's on his way. He's cleared it with his precinct captain and is bringing several detectives. He also notified the medical examiner. I'll send our boat to get him," Johnson said. "The rangers are in the small conference room next to the administrative complex adjoining my office."

Johnson and I walked ahead of the others. He reiterated what he told me on the phone, adding some embellishments and becoming more animated as he went on. When we arrived at the administration building, he sent a ranger to wait at the dock for Torre. William Johnson wasn't afraid to make tough decisions. He was totally committed to protecting the Statue of Liberty.

Torre and three detectives appeared within minutes of my arrival. Each wore a sports jacket, white shirt and tie, and chino slacks. Torre was dressed differently. He needed a shave. The frayed button down collar of his light blue oxford shirt was open. A maroon and dark blue striped tie hung loosely from his neck. His dark gray slacks and gray tweed sports jacket needed a pressing and the black penny loafers needed new heels and a good coat of shoe polish. Torre held a half-smoked cigarette.

Johnson grabbed a ring of keys from his desk and led us to a larger room next door. When we were seated around the large conference table, he told us who was on the island when the body was discovered, and what he had done since the Park Police were notified.

"I'm single so I occupy one of the several housing units on the Island. I'm generally the first person on duty in the morning."

"I thought you have security on duty throughout the night," a detective interrupted.

"We do. Rangers with law enforcement commissions are on duty twenty-four hours a day. I mean administrative staff. I'm the highest-ranking island resident so I make the hard decisions in emergencies after hours."

"What time is that?" he was asked.

"Generally five-thirty or six o'clock in the afternoon, sometimes a little bit later, depending on how many people there are on the island. We begin clearing thirty to sixty minutes before the last ferry and we also conduct a thorough sweep of the monument itself after the last ferry leaves." Johnson continued.

"Do the concession people leave on the last ferry?"

"Usually the concession closes about twenty minutes before the last boat. Supervisors take the Park Service boat to Manhattan or Jersey City. Within an hour after the last ferries leave, the only persons on the island are the night rangers and residents."

The deputy chief ranger then explained his daily routine.

"I like to be in my office by seven and usually go over my messages and unfinished business from the night before. I try to meet briefly with the night supervisor before he or she goes home. I then go to the monument, unlock it, and walk around inside. Sometimes I like to play tourist. Would you believe I learn something new every time I'm in the building?" Johnson suddenly smiled.

"Yesterday was crazy. We were busier than a one armed paperhanger. Ya know, lost kids, people complaining about the lines, thousands of questions like where's the bathroom or the souvenir stand, comments about the hot temperatures, the usual bullshit. It was like Murphy's Law. Everything that could go wrong did and my staff and I were dragging ass. I must've been pretty tired because I was asleep by ten last night and must've slept through the alarm this morning. In fact, the TV was on when I got up so I must've dozed off during the ten o'clock news. That's very unusual for me. So I took my time showering and shaving. Instead of the usual quick bite to eat, I made myself a good breakfast. Eggs and toast and an extra cup of coffee…The whole nine yards." He then pointed to his office next door.

"There was a lot of paperwork I didn't get to. Besides, I just told you that I was tired so I did what I don't ordinarily do. I decided to have Jennifer Marcus take over for me and inspect the Statue before the morning crew came on board. Jennifer was one of the rangers working the night security staff. I called her into my office, explained the routine, and what I do each morning."

"How'd she react?" Torre asked.

"Fine, although I got the impression she was nervous at the thought of being the only one in the entire monument. I told her the whole inspection takes no more than a half-hour under normal circumstances. Who knew there was a dead body lying on the second landing? Honest, guys, I wasn't aware of the corpse. You can bet the farm that if I knew about the body, I sure as Hell wouldn't have sent anyone, especially Jennifer, into the monument. I would've been on the phone to you earlier." Johnson stared at me. He removed his glasses and wiped them with a handkerchief he had removed from his back pocket.

"What time does the shift change?" Torre asked.

"The Park Service boat makes a run at six and another at seven-thirty. There's also a later boat at nine. Sometimes a ranger from the night staff stays longer to chow in the concession area when it opens, and take a regular ferry back to the mainland," he added.

"Why'd anybody who spent the night here wanna stay after normal working hours? I'd think he'd want to be off the island as soon as possible," Torre asked Johnson.

"Sometimes there's paperwork, sometimes they're in the middle of a project or they want to polish their shoes, make phone calls or do any kinda personal chores. We're not supposed to make personal calls on government phones but everyone ignores that regulation. We don't keep a log of long-distance calls. It's considered one of the few perks. Then there are those individuals who have late morning appointments in Manhattan and don't want to take two subways and pay the extra fare to go home first, so they stay later. Or they want to discuss something with someone coming on duty. It's also not difficult to just miss the staff run. I could think of more reasons why they'd not be on the park boat," Johnson responded.

"So when you called Miss Marcus and instructed her to check the Statue of Liberty, what didja tell her to do?" Torre asked him.

"As I explained a minute ago, just walk through the monument and make a final check. Make sure maintenance cleaned it and removed any gum wrappers and things like that, check that the trash receptacles have been emptied, the brass has been polished and there are no burned out light bulbs. Just make sure the guys on maintenance did their jobs," Johnson said.

"Do ya do that often? I mean assign someone else to do the inspection?"

"No. This was the first time in several months; at least that I can remember. I enjoy doing it and except when I've been away from the island on vacation or for training I always make it a point to do it myself," Johnson answered.

I asked the deputy chief ranger to tell us what he knew about Jennifer Marcus.

"Jennifer joined the staff in visitor services. She then decided she wanted a law enforcement commission so she applied for appointment to the Federal Law Enforcement Training Institute in Georgia. When she graduated, she returned to New York City and joined the law enforcement ranger staff. Jen's a good ranger. We've never had any complaints about her. In fact, we get complimentary letters about her all the time. She recently asked to be assigned to the night shift. I don't know about any problems with her co-workers, at least that I'm aware of." Johnson again looked in my direction. "If Ron knows something about her, he hasn't told me."

"Who's Ron?" Torre asked.

"Ron Gaines. He's the chief ranger here. He's in charge of security and he's my boss. I report directly to him," Johnson explained.

I asked how many rangers were on duty the night before.

"About a half dozen," Johnson said.

"I assume with the exception of Ms Marcus, the other rangers are men. Why'd you pick this Marcus woman to inspect the Statue?" I asked.

"I really can't answer that, lieutenant. By the way, there's another woman ranger on night shift. Since I wasn't up to doing it myself this morning, I guess I had to assign someone and Jennifer was the first one that came to mind. There *is* no answer. Are you thinking…?"

I was taken aback by Johnson's formality in calling me lieutenant.

"What did *you* do while she was inside the Statue?" Torre asked. His facial expression hadn't changed since he walked into the room.

"After Jennifer…Ms Marcus, left my office, I walked into the hall and made small talk with our dispatcher about last night's Mets loss to the Braves. I then went back to my office to do some paperwork. Oh yeah. I also checked my computer for the daily reports from our regional office and Washington on e-mail. That's when I heard Jennifer radioing for help."

I asked Johnson how much time had elapsed from the time he assigned Jennifer Marcus to inspect the monument and the time she radioed for assistance.

"About twenty to twenty-five minutes."

"Would that be a normal amount of time, d'ya think, for her to have found the body after you gave her instructions?" I asked.

"She could've been taking her time. Twenty to thirty minutes is about right, as I already told you. She seemed scared. I know I was when I was in the Statue of Liberty alone for the first time. It takes time to get used to the loneliness, so I guess she took her time and did things slowly and methodically. Ya know, every footstep echoes and magnifies the fright and nervousness," Johnson said.

I asked the deputy chief ranger to try to remember her exact words. He sat back in his chair. His fingers were hooked in the form of an arch while his elbows rested on the table. He then stroked his dark brown chin with his right hand as if weighing each word carefully. His eyes wandered around the room. I tried to read something in his facial expressions. From the stares of the others, I got the impression they were searching for something, too.

"She repeated herself several times before I could respond. She identified herself by her call numbers. She repeated the call numbers two or three times. She was very agitated. Then I started to feel my hands shake. All she said was that it was an emergency. I was totally scared, probably more scared than she was since I didn't know whether she was in any immediate danger. I remember I asked myself what coulda gone wrong. 'Of all the Goddamned mornings to send her into the Statue. What did I do that for and what kind of friggin' mess is she in?' When I radioed back, she repeated that there was an emergency but did not elaborate," Johnson said.

"Did she say or hint she was in any danger?" I asked.

Johnson nodded in the negative.

"What happened next?" I asked.

"She pleaded for me to send help right away."

"Didja ask if she was in danger?" Torre asked.

Johnson showed signs of irritation for the first time since our arrival.

"I just told you she volunteered that she wasn't in any danger before I could ask her. But I couldn't be sure of that. I wasn't convinced she wasn't in some sort of trouble. To be honest with you, I was

Goddamned frightened. I didn't know what to think. She could've fallen and gotten hurt. Someone hiding in the monument could've held a gun to her head. Who knew what was going on?"

"What kinda trouble did you expect?" Torre asked.

"I ain't lyin' to you. I sure as Hell didn't know. I told you guys before. In all my years here, this was the first time there's been any murder. All I knew was that a ranger who'd gone through the Federal Law Enforcement Training School, carried a pistol in her holster, and was trained to handle just about any kind of emergency, shouldn't have had to radio for help at that hour of the morning in an empty monument unless she was in some real trouble. She wouldn't call to report there was an emergency if there was something she could handle routinely." There was a momentary pause.

"Again, what was your first reaction?" Torre asked once more.

"This was totally unlike her and who woulda known what was going on? No one expected anyone else to be in the building when she got there. How could they have gotten in?" Johnson's eyes were riveted on those of the veteran New York City detective sergeant. He spoke as if trying to read Vince Torre's mind. Torre did not react.

"So what did you do next?" I asked.

"I jumped up and checked my waist for my holster and revolver. I didn't bother to look for my hat but ran out of the office and out of the building. I shouted for Bernie...He's the dispatcher...to radio the other rangers to meet me at the second landing where Jennifer was radioing from."

Torre took a black leather-covered note pad from the pocket of his sports jacket and jotted down some notes with an inexpensive ballpoint pen. Johnson continued to talk. The deputy chief ranger suddenly stood and put his hands on his waist.

"I'm about forty pounds more than I was when I graduated from the police academy. But I ran out the door just the same. My holster was bouncing against my shin and it hurt like a son of a bitch. I ran and I stumbled on the brick path in front of the monument. One of the other rangers helped me up and we ran together the rest of the way." Johnson described his panic but said he told himself to keep going and don't quit.

"I continued to justify assigning Jennifer Marcus to open it. I worried about what shape or condition she would be in when we got to her. Frankly, I was concerned about her safety and whether we'd find her alive. I was becoming desperate"

Torre continued to take notes. He said nothing.

"When I got to the door, I fell against it. The doors are heavy suckers and Jennifer had locked them from the inside, so I grabbed for my keys. Before I could unlock the door, one of the other rangers behind me unlocked it. I was out of breath and out of shape. My adrenaline was flowing like grape juice and I staggered inside."

I noticed Johnson was beginning to sweat so I told him to take another break. He again removed his handkerchief from his back pocket and wiped his face, apologizing for his condition. The room remained silent. I looked around the room but still couldn't detect any reaction. Torre displayed his eternal poker face. I remember telling myself that either Johnson was the dedicated employee I always thought he was or he was one good actor...Or liar. I wanted to believe the former and hoped that I was right. But as a cop, I was also a realist and couldn't rule him out as a suspect.

"Sorry guys," Johnson said. "Where was I? Oh yeah. I staggered into the Statue and leaned against the brass railing around the old torch in the lower lobby to catch my breath. I was wiped out and I remember saying I'm too old for this crap. Then I ran up the steps to the second landing. The other rangers were already there by the time I got there. One of the guys had his arm around Jennifer. I felt relieved that she wasn't in danger but I could see her chest pounding like a bass drum. She didn't say anything. She just sat cross-legged on the floor and just pointed to the body. I sat down next to her. My shirt was like a sponge and I was shivering."

"Go on," Torre said.

"I assigned two rangers to walk around the monument to check everything. I ordered them to carry their two-way radios and to make certain their gun holsters were unsnapped in case they needed them. I then instructed everyone else to leave and warned them not to go near or touch the body or anything else until the Park Police were notified."

"What happened with Ms Marcus?"

"I had Jennifer stay with me since I wasn't sure of her mental state and wanted to keep an eye on her. I radioed the dispatcher and had him call the superintendent. I guess he also called the commander who called you," Johnson said as he looked in my direction.

"Then what didja do?" Torre asked.

"I checked the dead woman's pulse. Not a beat. I waited for the two rangers to return and when I was assured the monument was secure, we all left."

"Did you secure the interior?" a detective asked.

"Yeah. I personally made sure the doors were locked. I'll bet my life no one's been in the building since we left. I'll guarantee it," he said.

Johnson was asked who knew about the body and he repeated the list of people he called.

"What didja tell 'em?" Torre asked. The detective had closed his note pad and put it and his pen onto the table. He had one leg crossed over the other and was leaning one elbow on his thigh, bent forward to catch everything Johnson said.

"I called the superintendent and apparently woke him. When Sam…"

"Who's Sam?" he was interrupted.

"Sorry about that. I thought you knew him. Sam Belmont, the superintendent. I told him about the corpse and everything I told you except that I didn't go into as much detail." Johnson reiterated that he then called the ferry line and Gaines.

Johnson was asked to describe the victim and what she wore. He said she looked like she was in her mid-twenties and was wearing tight faded but clean jeans and a plaid red, white and green blouse open at the neck. Her sneakers looked new and her clothes were intact."

"Did you check for bruises?"

"I did. I didn't check her body, only the exposed parts. There were no obvious bruises on her face or arms or neck, there was no sign of blood on her denims, and her clothing was not in disarray. She looked like she was in a deep sleep."

I assigned officers to search the monument and the grounds. Within minutes, Park Police were photographing and measuring the entire crime scene and dusting for fingerprints throughout the second landing. I didn't expect the fingerprints to turn up anything.

I then told Johnson to send in Ms Marcus so that Torre and I could question her. I also asked for personnel records of everyone on the island the night before.

"That includes you and Gaines." I said. I expected trouble from Gaines and wanted as much information about him as I could get.

Chapter 2

"C'mon Ron. Where are you? Answer the friggin' phone..."

William Johnson alternately sat and stood in his small office. He grasped the phone tightly in his left hand while he anxiously tapped the top of his wooden desk with the eraser of a wooden pencil. He stared blankly at the wall clock in front of him as its second hand crept slowly around the face while he waited impatiently for his boss to answer the phone.

Johnson knew that under normal circumstances, the chief ranger would be asleep, having worked the previous weekend. He knew, too, that Gaines was a heavy sleeper and if his wife wasn't at home, he may not have heard the phone. That's why he didn't hang up. After several rings, however, he became annoyed.

Gaines *had* heard phone ring. It *had* disturbed his sleep. But he didn't give a damn who was trying to reach him. Just as he enjoyed intimidating others, he got a kick out of keeping callers on the line. They could call back later if it was important. He couldn't be bothered accommodating anyone on his day off. He knew he'd never win a personality contest and that just about the entire National Park Service knew it. Sometimes Gaines even wondered how or why his wife and young children put up with him.

Gaines got tired of the ringing and finally grabbed for the phone.

"Yeah."

"Ron..."

"Wha...What time is it? Who...Who...Who's calling?" Gaines mumbled into the beige receiver.

"It's me...It's William Johnson. You'd better wake up, damn it."

Gaines knew that Johnson never called him early in the morning so that something serious had taken place that needed his attention. He was suddenly fully awake.

"What's going on? What time d'ya have?"

"It's close to eight in the morning. I think there's been a homicide. We have a dead body lying on the second level of the monument."

"Say that again. Pass it by me one more time. You got a what? What did you smoke last night?"

"I didn't smoke anything." Johnson related the details.

"Were there signs of violence?"

"No. The woman was just lyin' there real peaceful like." Gaines asked what else was found. His deputy said nothing.

There was a pause.

"Who else knows about this?"

"I called the superintendent and Lieutenant Mike Finnegan."

"Goddamnit. This island's *our* responsibility. The city cops and fuckin' Park Police don't get involved unless we call them. The superintendent should know that. I'll take care of it, even if I have to kick some ass myself."

"Godamnit to Hell and back to you, you stupid son of a bitch. Cool it, Ron. The superintendent told me to contact the Park Police. Frankly, I don't blame him. Climb down from your horse, man. There's political implications here. The world will know about this in a few hours. How do you expect us to muster up the resources to investigate this case? If you want my opinion, I'm glad the cops are involved. At least *we* won't have to answer to the politicians. Let the cops do it. If something goes wrong or it takes too long, it ain't our fault. If you've got something against that, get off the phone and call Sam yourself. Don't let off steam at me. I followed procedures. The final decision to call the cops was his," Johnson shouted.

Gaines suddenly sat upright. His long legs hung over the side and his toes rested on the carpeted bedroom floor. There were several seconds of silence as he listened intently. He pondered what his friend and deputy told him. He remained silent.

"I suggest you get your damned butt down here to see for yourself. I don't like this any more than you do, Ron, but let's face it. This is beyond our ability to deal with. Somewhere down the line we'd need to call in the cops anyway. How in the world can we conduct a fair investigation if one of our people may be involved? Cool it, man. Just cool it."

Although the air conditioning fan in the bedroom was set on high, the chief ranger wiped perspiration from his face with the sleeve of his pajama top.

"Describe the body for me. How old d'ya think she was? What did she look like? What was she wearing? How tall was she?" As he spoke, Gaines felt his throat go dry. His pajama top, like the rest of his body, was drenched.

"Why are you peppering me with all these questions?"

"None of your business. I don't have to explain everything I do or say."

"La de da da. King Tut himself. Excuse me for bothering you, your royal highness," Johnson shouted back.

Gaines calmed down.

"All I do know is that you'd better get down here pronto."

Gaines slammed down the receiver and contemplated what to do next. His wife Lorelei had told him Sunday night that she was taking their two young children to visit her mother so that he could sleep in Monday morning. She left a list of things she wanted him to do. The sleep and the chores would have to wait.

Ron Gaines hastily jumped out of bed, showered and shaved.

Several highly starched green and gray Park Service uniforms hung neatly in his bedroom closet, but he chose a sweatshirt and jeans.

Gaines grabbed an apple from the refrigerator. He wrote his wife a note and left the house to begin the drive back to catch the Park Service boat to Liberty Island. He was no longer in control of the situation and of his emotions. For the first time in several years, he was truly frightened and angry. He turned on the pickup truck's radio and flipped the dial from the soft rock music station he usually listened to until he found one of the twenty-four-hour all-news stations. When the anchors began to recycle the news after about twenty minutes, Gaines knew the murder had not leaked to the press. He wondered whether Johnson's call was a nightmare or a figment of his imagination. He would soon find out.

Johnson eased the phone back onto its cradle. He felt sorry for his boss. He knew that Gaines was seeing other women and that his gambling habit consumed much of his pay. Lorelei Gaines, however, accepted her husband's excuses for the frequent absences from home. Since Gaines had his pay stubs mailed to his office, his wife never saw them. He blamed being short of cash on increased taxes and rising costs for health insurance. Lorelei Gaines was embarrassed to always ask her parents for money. She apologized that her husband's pay didn't keep up with inflation. She had little choice. Her parents always helped her.

Gaines had graduated from college when the Vietnam War broke out. He fled to Canada in order to avoid the draft. That decision left emotional scars. He returned to the States when the President issued a general amnesty to draft evaders but by then it was too late.

"My father said he never wanted to see me again, that bastard. When my kid brother was killed in that fucking war, there was no chance of reconciliation. That was it. It's a cross I've got to bear to my grave. I don't give a damn. If they don't like it, that's their problem and not mine. I beat the draft but I'm no coward," Gaines once confided to Johnson. Gaines attended the Federal Law Enforcement Academy, received a commission, and eventually moved to Liberty Island as its chief ranger. He started popping heavy doses of anti-depressants shortly after his arrival in New York.

Gaines at first opposed Johnson's appointment as his deputy.

"Is he one of those guys who's here on account of his color? I need a guy to make tough decisions. Not some guy who's here to fill a quota," Gaines told the superintendent. He was overruled.

William Johnson served with a combat infantry unit in Vietnam. At first, he and Gaines argued every day about America's involvement. They quickly realized they needed each other's support. They became good working partners. After several heated debates, the war was rarely discussed. Whenever Lorelei Gaines called and her husband wasn't there, Johnson made up an excuse.

Johnson worked his way through a small black college in North Carolina that awarded him a baseball scholarship. The Pittsburgh Pirates drafted him after graduation and assigned him to a minor league affiliate. He gave up baseball to enlist in the Army and earned the Purple Heart and Silver Star for wounds and bravery in combat. Following lengthy hospitalization in a Veterans Administration Hospital, he fully recovered. The painkillers prescribed by Army doctors, however, led to a serious drug dependency.

He returned to North Carolina where he found a job in the office of a large furniture manufacturing firm outside High Point. His drug habit left little money for food and he was able to barely cover the rent for his small apartment.

March 15, 1979 changed his life. A co-worker invited him to lunch. They occupied a table in a quiet section of a small neighborhood diner.

"Look Will. I gotta talk to you man-to-man. We're the only brothers in the office. You know why they hired us."

"What kind of stupid question is that? Because we're veterans," Johnson responded.

"Bullshit! Wise up, man. They hired us on accounta they need token brothers. Ya know. We're helping the boss get some lucrative government contracts because he's doing what they call diversifying. Get my drift?"

"No shit?"

"Yeah, Willie. That's the way it is, man."

"There's nothing wrong with that as long as we got jobs. Why're you telling me this?"

"Listen, Willie. You Goddamned coke head."

"Whatcha talking about?" Johnson tried to act nonchalant.

"Look Johnson. I don't give a rat's ass what you do in your own time. Everybody around here knows you're into that heavy stuff and it's making guys like you and me look bad. You gotta make up your mind and go clean. You ain't helping me and you ain't helping yourself. And you sure as Hell ain't helping your brothers. You're a druggie and it reflects bad on all of us."

Johnson stared at his friend. He cupped his dark brown hands over his face and began to sob. His friend walked to a pay phone near the cashier's counter and called the office.

"William Johnson isn't feeling well. I think it's serious. I'm taking him to a doctor so I won't be back the rest of the day. Charge it as emergency vacation time. I'll explain tomorrow morning."

Johnson was driven to a Veterans Administration hospital forty-five minutes away. The following morning the furniture company granted him a medical leave of absence.

William Johnson overcame his drug dependency with the support of the medical staff and his outpatient psychotherapist. The therapist later wrote a memo for Johnson's file that she had never seen as much determination as he had displayed. She advised him to leave High Point. Her patient complied and he never looked back.

He applied for a position as a Park Service ranger at the Everglades National Park in Florida. His employment chances were bolstered because he was a college-educated African-American with a ten-point veteran's credit resulting from his war-related injuries. His record did not mention that his therapist called an influential friend in Washington, D. C. on his behalf.

Johnson remained clean of drugs since leaving North Carolina. He even avoided cigarettes and acted as an anti-tobacco missionary. He did develop one other addiction, however. He became a devout believer in God. That's why he took the first Park Service boat to Manhattan in order to attend early church services every Sunday morning. He had survived the Vietnam War, he overcame prejudice and a drug problem. He learned to tolerate Ron Gaines. William Johnson knew that Someone of a Higher Authority was looking down on him.

CHAPTER 3

"What do you think?" I asked Torre.

"I ain't got no clue. We just gotta wait and see," Torre said matter-of-factly.

"If ya want my opinion. Just off the top of my head, mind ya. I ain't rulin' no one out who was on the island last night," he added

The police sergeant pulled a package of unfiltered cigarettes from his shirt pocket. Reaching into the side pocket of the jacket, he retrieved an old Zippo lighter and lit the cigarette.

The wife's been naggin' me to quit but I can't. What's the use? If I ain't died yet from this stuff, I'll live to be a hundred."

A gentle knock on the door interrupted our conversation.

"Come on in," I shouted. It was Jennifer Marcus. She was attractive. You know, blonde hair down to her shoulders. The drab Park Service uniform did not hide her nice figure. She began to blush. If I hadn't known what she had gone through that morning, I never would have guessed she discovered a dead body only hours before.

The young woman smiled and asked if she could come in.

"William Johnson said you want to speak to me," she said apologetically. She stood waiting to be introduced to Sergeant Torre.

The detective got up and ground out his cigarette in an ashtray at the center of the table. He extended his hand and then pointed to the table.

Jennifer Marcus sat opposite us, her hands resting on her lap. She waited silently for us to start the conversation. She seemed to be very reserved and relaxed. I explained that the superintendent asked the Park Police to handle the investigation and that I requested Sergeant Torre's assistance.

"I know it was painful finding the body. But please describe in your own words what took place from the time you got the call from William Johnson to inspect the Statue of Liberty." Her story was pretty much the way Johnson explained it earlier. I was getting so I knew it from memory.

"Didja ever open the monument before this morning?" Torre asked.

"No."

"To the best of your knowledge, Miss Marcus, who's usually the first one in the monument in the morning?"

"Usually it's my boss Will Johnson…At least when I'm working nights. I can't tell you what happens on my days off. William takes his job seriously. He really loves this place. He can take a joke, though, and one of us is always kidding him to get a life. There are other women in this world besides the Statue of Liberty," the ranger said. I detected a smile on her face.

"Does Will Johnson have any girlfriends?"

"Not that I am aware of." She began to think about where this line of questioning was going. She displayed signs of displeasure.

"What can you tell us about the chief ranger? What's his name? Ron Gaines?" Torre asked.

"We don't want you to tell us nuttin' personal. Please tell us your general observations. I remind you that Gaines and Johnson and you are not suspects. We gotta ask these questions. They're all part of our investigation."

"I know and appreciate that. But does that mean that you'll ask Will and Ron what they know about me?" Her face turned serious.

"Maybe."

"I don't know too much about Will. He's a straight shooter, a regular guy, and we all like working for him. You never doubt what he means or where he's coming from." I detected a southern drawl.

"Where are you from? You sound like you're from the South. Am I correct?"

"Alabama. Just outside of Birmingham. My family still lives there."

Torre asked her to describe Ron Gaines. There was hesitation.

"Ron's an OK guy. Not as easygoing as Will but we tolerate him. Although he shouts a lot, I think he's harmless. He has a job to do and we respect it. Will's easier to work with since you can get close to him."

"Did you ever have a disagreement with Gaines? Did he ever pick on you?"

"Not that I can recall."

"What d'ya mean by Gaines being 'an OK guy'?"

The park ranger's face reddened.

"I object to where this questioning is going. I don't mind answering any questions relating to this investigation. I must tell you gentlemen, however, that I am extremely uncomfortable giving you my personal observations about anyone else, in particular my supervisors. I can't speak for them and I refuse to do so. I'd rather not say anything else on this subject, if that's fine with you."

Torre nodded. I didn't pursue the issue either.

I asked her some innocuous questions about her job, finding the body, her life and how she liked New York City. I felt I needed to know where she was coming from.

She did volunteer some information.

"I earned a degree in drama from the University of Alabama and decided to come to New York to pursue a career on the stage. I couldn't find work immediately so I took some part-time jobs. When I heard in 1989 that they were going to open Ellis Island as a museum, I called the superintendent and requested an interview. Maybe it was ballsy on my part but I had nothing to lose. I outlined what I had in mind. I wanted to develop visitor programs for kids and school groups."

Jennifer Marcus was quiet. She pondered telling the detectives that Ron Gaines had told her about the museum one night when they were smoking pot and making love in her Greenwich Village apartment. She said nothing.

"What happened next?" Torre asked.

"The superintendent called me in early 1990 to offer me a job. He put my original ideas for programs on hold. Since I needed a steady paycheck, I accepted the job offer. My activities included giving tours, answering questions, and developing programs for school groups. During the summer, I dealt with visitor control and information."

"You seem people-oriented," I said.

"If that's meant as a compliment, thank you. You are very discerning, lieutenant. I am and continue to be."

Torre stared at the wall behind Miss Marcus. He gently tapped his pen on the tabletop.

"You look like something's bothering you, Sergeant Torre. Did I say something that confused you?"

"Yeah. You like people. So how come you chose to work nights where there's only a handful of rangers and no one else to talk to? The apparent contradiction's got me perplexed," Torre said.

"That's easy. I figured that as a woman I had to try harder. You men don't know the feeling. When we take a new job and advance in our careers, it's because we slept around with the right people. If we fail, it's because women can't handle it. Everything is categorized by gender. It's not fair. I was determined to prove myself as a person and not as a woman."

"So you applied for law enforcement training?" Torre interrupted.

"Yes. I felt I had to develop as many skills as I could. School was tough."

"You haven't answered my question, Miss Marcus. Why'd you decide to work nights? It's none of my business. But don't you have a social life?"

"You don't understand, sergeant. I had to prove something. There were several women in my law enforcement training class. I had to be one step better than they are. Working nights when there's no one around the island but a half dozen of us poses a challenge. It's got more potential risk. Suppose something was to happen? A terrorist trying to storm the island, or an explosion..."

"Or a homicide, Miss Marcus..." Torre again interrupted.

"Yes. Even an unexplained death, sergeant. There's only a handful of us. Don't you see what I'm trying to explain? It's me. I've got to always be a step ahead of the pack. It may sound corny and trite. But that's the way it is. I've always been different. Go where women didn't go and do what my gender was afraid to do. When I succeed, I want men to say I did it on my own and not on my back. If you don't accept that, I'm sorry. Besides, it doesn't look bad on my resume if I ever want to leave here," she said. She stared at us for a moment and smiled.

Since we both were graduates from the same law enforcement program, I told her we had something in common. She smiled again. This was the opening; the common denominator to keep Jennifer Marcus at ease and relieve any tension that was developing. I, therefore, reminisced on how the academy was when I went there, asked about her instructors, the living conditions, and the rigorous physical training.

"It was hard, especially for a woman. I was insane. I really pushed myself. As I said, I thought the law enforcement commission would provide greater career opportunities in other parks. I felt the commission would add to my experience in a positive way. Before the academy my promotion opportunities were too limited."

Jennifer Marcus paused. She looked at Torre and me. Damnit she has pretty eyes, I said to myself.

"You know, lieutenant, I want to be an all-around person with many skills."

"Do you plan to leave New York?" I asked her.

"After what happened to me this morning, I must admit I have some second thoughts about using my law enforcement commission in an isolated park. Just between the three of us, I was scared out of my wits when I found the body. The first thing I asked myself is what I was doing here?"

"You really didn't answer my question. Are you considering leaving here?"

"Anything is possible. Not immediately, though. I don't have any plans to leave. I haven't seen any job announcements that really appeal to me," she added.

Our meeting had become, at least for the moment, a friendly dialogue. I didn't know how much longer I could keep it going.

"Would you move on if you saw a job elsewhere that you like?" Torre asked.

"I enjoyed Liberty Island until this morning," she said.

"You look like you've recovered pretty well," I told her. She smiled.

"I guess you were a good student at the academy." She responded that her acting training taught her to keep her personal feelings pretty much in control usually. I asked if she had any thoughts about who the woman might be or how or why she was in the monument. I again detected a bit of hesitancy before the ranger answered in the negative. Maybe it was that momentary pause, my instincts, or my experience as a police officer, but I sensed that Jennifer Marcus wasn't telling us everything she knew. I made a mental note for future reference.

I decided to change the subject and asked her what staff responsibilities were during the evening. She explained the various functions. Regular patrols of the island to make certain no intruders had accessed the island by boat, checks several times to make sure the doors to the monument were locked, and, rotating shifts at the switchboard and monitors at the administration desk.

Torre asked her to elaborate on the monitors. Jennifer Marcus explained that video cameras were strategically placed throughout the interior of the Statue. Monitors at the administration desk gave the ranger on duty a view of all areas of the structure at all times.

"What about interacting with the other rangers?" I asked.

"We all get along well and there's always something to talk about. Some of us are more conscientious than others. We're usually studying law enforcement techniques, first aid, CPR, and other procedures."

Torre suddenly came to life.

"Ya just told us if you're sitting at the front desk you can see what's going on anywhere in the monument. Correct?"

The ranger nodded in the affirmative.

Torre pointed his pencil into the air in a non-menacing way.

"How then could that woman hide if you could see everything on the TV monitors? Kindly explain, Miss Marcus."

The young ranger smiled back at him. She raised her palms upward.

"I don't know. One of us is always at the desk. If we have to go to the bathroom or want to go outside for a cigarette, there's always someone to take our place. We rotate stints at the monitors throughout the night. I really can't answer your question. If I knew that, perhaps I could have prevented a death. It sure is a mystery to me, sergeant. And please put that pencil down. It's making me nervous," she said with a smile.

Torre apologized and again put the pencil on the table. Since neither Vince Torre nor I had any further questions, we told Miss Marcus she could leave the island and that we'd get back to her if we needed more information as the investigation progressed. I admonished her to go home and get a good rest. She responded that my suggestion reminded her of what her father would say.

After she left, Torre asked what I knew about Gaines. I was explaining my previous dealings with him when we were interrupted by another knock on the door. This one was louder than the previous one.

"Who is it?" I shouted.

"The chief ranger."

"It's Gaines," I whispered. I yelled that the door was unlocked.

Ron Gaines was all spit and polish. His trousers had a sharp crease. His uniform shirt was heavily starched and the toes of his cordovan cowboy boots bore a mirror-like finish. Although the temperature had risen to the high nineties outside the building, he looked as if he just stepped out of a refrigerator. He was tense and I detected concern on his face. I introduced him to Torre and pointed to one of the chairs, inviting him to sit down.

"I'm the chief ranger here. In case you gentlemen aren't aware of protocol, I'm in charge of law enforcement."

"I heard a lot about ya. What can we do for ya?" Torre asked, his thick New York accent providing a deep contrast to Gaines' upper Midwestern dialect.

Gaines' face turned bright crimson. He was pissed off and didn't expect to be challenged. I remained silent. I expected the sergeant to put on an Academy Award performance and he didn't let me down. He was one of those old-fashioned cops who earned a reputation for skirting the regulations and doing whatever he thought he had to in order to solve a crime. He was brought up on charges several years earlier, in fact, after complaints by the American Civil Liberties Union that he had threatened physical force to intimidate a burglary suspect. The suspect eventually confessed that he had made up the story about Torre who was cleared of all charges.

Gaines snorted loudly.

"In case I didn't make myself clear, gentlemen, let me repeat. I am the chief ranger. I'm responsible for all law enforcement activities on this island. When I'm not here, my deputy assumes that responsibility after clearing with me. I believe you have met William Johnson? I am prepared to take over the investigation and want it on the record that I have not authorized your involvement. I will be more than happy to seek your guidance as the investigation develops. However, since law enforcement and security here are the responsibilities of National Park Service rangers, until such time as I request assistance, I will be the person in charge. Let me remind you, gentlemen, that Park Police and New York Police are called in *only* when I think it is appropriate. That is my decision. Those are the regulations on which my decision is based. It will continue to be. There will be no deviation. Do I make myself clear? Therefore, I must ask under what authority are you taking control without first clearing it with or going through me? My men and women are capable of handling any and all incidents that take place on Liberty Island. Unless or until I'm consulted, you are acting in an unofficial capacity. Again, do I make myself understood? Are there any questions?"

Torre slowly ground the remains of his cigarette into the small ashtray. He stared silently at the chief ranger. The detective suddenly became animated. He jumped to his feet, leaning across the table towards Gaines. He had picked up the pencil and pointed it within inches of the stunned chief ranger's nose.

"Listen to me, you little shit. You got no fuckin' authority to invite us in or tell us to get out. You bag of turd. Your outburst was outta place. I'll ignore it this time. You can consider this your lucky fuckin' day on accounta I ain't thrown *you* out on your behind. You gotta learn respect for your elders, young man."

"Who in Hell is your speechwriter? He's pretty good. He did one fine job. As far as I'm concerned, you and Lieutenant Finnegan have no authority over law enforcement activities on Liberty Island. Your tirade means nothing," Gaines persisted.

Torre walked slowly around the rooms, his hands hooked behind his back. He stared at the floor and said nothing. We waited in silence for his next outburst. We didn't have to wait long. Torre walked back to where he had been sitting. He rested his hands on the back of the armchair and leaned forward. He spoke softly.

"I can't help it if you got a beef with our bein' here. If your poor little ego is shattered, that's too fuckin' bad. Call the superintendent. Maybe your Congressman can help ya. In case ya didn't know it, there's been a mysterious death on Liberty Island. We have reason to believe it was a homicide. Yeah. I said homicide. Ask your assistant to lend ya a dictionary if you don't know what the word homicide means. Look under 'murder.' Murder, in case you don't know it, starts with the letter M." Torre's voice grew louder.

"For the record, turd face, every one of your rangers includin' you, ya disgustin' piece of shit, and your assistant William Johnson, and Ms Marcus who found the body, are suspects until we prove otherwise. Johnson and Ms Marcus have been very helpful and cooperative. It wouldn't be a bad idea if you followed their example. Who in Hell are the rangers gonna investigate? Themselves? For all we know, maybe you know somethin' about the friggin' murder or done it yourself and you don't want us to know about it. Maybe you're coverin' someone else's ass. So keep your mouth shut unless we ask ya a question. C'peech?"

Gaines percolated with anger but remained silent.

"Another thing, Shithead, we got joint jurisdiction on this island and I was called in by Lieutenant Finnegan. The superintendent knows what we're doing here. He called the Park Police and his commander told the lieutenant over here to handle the investigation. Lieutenant Finnegan used his authority to call me. Got it? Got a problem with that? If so, state it now or shut your Goddamned mouth. Understand what I'm sayin' or do I have to write ya a fuckin' note?"

Gaines remained motionless.

"Don't take me personally, officer..."

"I've got thirty-one years as a New York City police officer; fifteen of 'em as a detective. I'm old enough to be this wise ass's father. And I gotta take this crap from him," Torre muttered to himself.

"Now let me try again. What can we do for ya?" he asked.

"I was called by my deputy, William Johnson and I..." There was a pause. "We felt that I should be included in the investigation," Gaines said sheepishly.

"I understand where you're coming from and that my people may be suspects. On the other hand, as chief ranger, I must be kept informed of what is happening and the status of the investigation. There's a chain of command that must be maintained for discipline purposes and for future reference. We cannot set a precedent," he said.

Torre had calmed down.

"Good. If you want my opinion, I don't give a shit about precedent, schmecident. We got a murder on our hands and a potential murderer runnin' around. We gotta solve it. Now that we fully understand each other, Lieutenant Finnegan and I are coordinatin' the investigation. You had six persons on duty last night, including Ms Marcus. William Johnson makes seven suspects, unless there's others who know somethin'. Let me repeat. Your deputy called the superintendent who called the Park Police and Lieutenant Finnegan called me. Maybe we should consider you suspect number eight. Now we ain't accusin' no one of nothin', mind you. But just for your information, we gotta consider everyone. Ya read me?"

"Yeah," Gaines said. He, too, had regained his composure.

"Tell us what you know," Torre said.

"All I know is what Johnson filled me in on when he woke me this morning. A body was found. So far there's no identification and cause of death. We don't know how or why she was in the Statue."

"A-plus," Torre said sarcastically. "Any ideas, thoughts or suspicions, Mr. Gaines?"

"No," the chief ranger replied.

Will Johnson had provided us with a copy of the duty roster from the night before. I showed it to Ron Gaines and asked if he could tell us if any of the names on the list might be pertinent to the investigation. Gaines studied the list and said he knew of nothing.

"They're all fine rangers," he said. Gaines then asked if there was anything he could do and we responded in the negative.

"We'll call you if we need your help," I said. Gaines left the room.

Torre and I looked at each other and laughed simultaneously.

* * *

Our officers returned from the Statue and brought back an assortment of items that could be found at any tourist attraction such as combs, pens, coins in various denominations, a wallet and someone's credit card. One detective found a brass screw not far from the body. This, like all the items, was put into manila envelopes and marked as to date and where it was found. There appeared to be nothing of substance. The medical examiner, meanwhile, examined the body and had the body removed to the morgue in Manhattan where an autopsy would be performed. We assigned detectives to do preliminary interviews with each of the rangers and left the island.

When I returned to the Park Police field office in Brooklyn, I filled in the chief on what had happened. I also asked to be relieved of all other assignments.

"I'll need more help. Can I have a blank check until I know where I'm going with this?"

I was given the manpower but no additional funds

* * *

The chief ranger walked into his office, slammed and locked the door. He sat and contemplated his next move. He swore to himself that he'd not give up control of Liberty Island without a fight. He then called his mother-in-law's home.

"Hi Mom, how're you doing? Are the grandchildren giving you a hard time?"

"Why Ronald. It's so nice of you to call. Is everything all right? You usually don't call in the morning when Lorelei and the children are here."

"Trust me, Mom. Everything is fine. I just have to speak to Lorelei for a second. It won't take long. I promise."

"Hi Hon. Is everything OK? You don't sound right."

"Listen, Lor. Will Johnson called me early this morning. He said there was an emergency at the Statue and he needed my help. I don't know what time I'll be home. Obviously I didn't get a chance to do the things on the list you left for me. They found a dead body inside the monument and..."

"What are you saying? Are you teasing me?"

"No. It's true. Will called in the New York Police and the Park Police. They insist that that I lead the investigation. I've got some good people helping me so I think we'll be fine. I'll probably stay in Manhattan for a few nights so I can be close to the action in case something develops. I promise I'll call every chance I get. Move in with your folks so that you won't be alone. I love you."

"Where will you stay in case I've got to get a hold of you?" Lorelei Gaines asked her husband.

"Leave a message at the Liberty Island dispatch office and I'll get back to you when I can. I'll probably stay at a different ranger's place every night. Don't want to take advantage of the staff's generosity. They're already fighting over me. I've got the best staff. If we ever transfer to another park, I'll make sure to try to bring them with me."

"That's wonderful. At least you don't have to worry about your subordinates. It speaks well for you, dear. I'm so proud of you," Lorelei responded.

Gaines stared at his wife's photograph.

Chapter 4

Shirley Konowitz was the product of a middle class environment in Boston. Her parents divorced when she was in her teens.

The divorce did irreparable harm to her psyche. Although college educated, with a master's degree in psychology, she couldn't find a job to her liking in Massachusetts so she moved to New York where she found an apartment in Greenwich Village and took temporary jobs while looking for a permanent placement.

Her father Sergei fled Poland in the 1940s to avoid certain death or worse in a concentration camp. He eventually stumbled upon an American military compound where the soldiers adopted him. The teenager was taught some English and was allowed to work around the compound where he ran errands, cleaned up, and did various chores.

He was allowed to accompany the American troops back to the States following the War. He moved in with a former corporal and his wife who shared a small apartment in the Bronx. They arranged for the young immigrant to attend evening classes to learn English and American history and he was helped to find a job washing dishes in a restaurant while studying for his American citizenship. He left the restaurant within a few months to take a job in a garment factory in

Manhattan. He then moved to Worcester, Massachusetts to become a cutter in a men's suit factory. He quickly moved up to foreman.

Sergie continued to work in the factory and enrolled in a local community college where he earned an associate's degree in business. Diploma in hand, he sought his fortune outside of Worcester and moved to Boston where he used up all his accumulated savings to open a small clothing store that consumed most of his time.

The business flourished and the new entrepreneur found time for other activities such as Rotary and a nearby synagogue… At a Sabbath service one Friday evening, a member of the temple introduced him to his daughter. A large wedding united Sergei Konowitz and Sophie Abramowitz, herself the daughter of Holocaust survivors. Shirley was born a year-and-a-half later and named for Sergei's mother who had perished in the Holocaust.

Shirley Konowitz developed strong sensitivities at a young age and a desire to help others. She shared her school lunch with another child who couldn't afford to buy one, and she asked her mother for extra milk money so that she could buy milk for classmates whose parents weren't as economically comfortable. She even helped friends with their homework, going to their homes after school to assist them when they found the lessons difficult. More than one parent noted that she would make an excellent schoolteacher.

She needed no coaxing to do her chores at home, making her bed, helping with the evening dishes, and bringing dinner to the store on Thursday night when her father stayed late. She was an only child but she was not spoiled.

After an uneventful four years spent in high school, where her grades were average and she was quite popular, Shirley Konowitz enrolled in a Boston university. Her social life as a freshman on campus was not spectacular. But neither was it dull. She lived in the dormitory and had her share of dates and fun evenings. By choice, however, she frequently remained alone to study. She dated several male students, nothing serious. When she really liked one, she would go to his apartment, off campus, for the evening.

Life seemed to change late in her second semester when she accepted an invitation to a Saturday night party at the apartment of a junior, an attractive woman from Providence. Several couples and some singles were there and after drinks, the usual hors d'oeuvres, and small talk, Shirley and the hostess found themselves alone in the small kitchen doing dishes.

"It's late. I'm afraid for you to go home alone," Sarah Ryan said as they wiped and put away some of the dishes left from the party.

"Don't worry about me. I'm OK. What can happen to me?" Shirley responded.

"No. I want you to stay. Remember that I know a little bit more than you do about life in the Big City. It's late. Freshmen don't walk the streets of Boston at one thirty in the morning," Sarah insisted.

"I'll take a cab. Where's your phone book?" Shirley countered.

"Nothing of the kind." Sarah tightly gripped Shirley's shoulders, turned her around, and stared her in the eyes.

Shirley Konowitz was temporarily hypnotized and convinced that Sarah was sincere and determined to look out for her. She admittedly was afraid to leave on her own but she didn't say anything. When the last dish was put away, the two young women sat, chatting and smoking in the small living room.

"Whew. It's warm. Wish the landlord would lower the heat. I'm stifling," Sarah said as she kicked off her shoes and opened the top two buttons of her blouse. Shirley couldn't help but notice the cleavage. The apartment *was* warm but she attributed it to the alcohol she had consumed earlier.

"Let me open the window," Shirley said as she rose from the sofa.

"No. The noise'll keep us awake. We'll survive. Take off your sweater if you want. It's just the two of us," Sarah said with a soft smile. She suddenly arose from the heavily padded armchair and patted her skirt as if looking for something.

"Now where did I put my cigarettes? I'll be back in a minute. I think I've got some in the bedroom."

A few minutes later, the hostess returned to the living room wearing only panties and a bra, which didn't hide her bosom and her beautiful figure.

"I hope you're not embarrassed. I always walk around the apartment this way when it's hot. Why don't you relax and make yourself comfortable. You can undress if you wish."

Shirley Konowitz was uncomfortable but it wasn't from the heat. She wanted to stay for the evening. However, her hostess intimidated her.

"I...I...I...think it's time to go to bed. It was a long day and a swell party and I'm pooped. I'll be better company in the morning," Shirley said.

The two women opened the sofa bed in which Shirley would spend the evening, or what was left of it.

"You can use the bathroom over there. I'll lend you a pair of pjs. I've got several pair in the other room," she said.

"I'm fine. I'll sleep in my underwear. I don't want to make more work for you," Shirley countered as she reluctantly slipped off her sweater and lowered her skirt and slip to the floor. Sarah Ryan lingered in the room watching her undress.

"If you don't mind, I'll use the bathroom to freshen up," Shirley was aware of the attention being shown by her hostess and was embarrassed by it.

"Great. I'll get some sheets and a pillow from the bedroom and make the bed while you're washing up."

When Shirley returned from the bathroom, the bed was already made up and Sarah Ryan was nowhere to be seen.

"Don't fall asleep on me now," the hostess shouted from the other room as Shirley climbed under the covers and closed her eyes. She was about to drift into a deep sleep when she was awakened by dark shadows over her bed. She looked up with a start.

"Only me, your big sister, coming to tuck you in for the night," Sarah Ryan whispered into Shirley's ear.

Sarah pulled the covers ever so gently over her sleeping guest, innocently rubbing the palm of her hand over Shirley's breast as she drew the covers tightly. She sat at the side of the sofa bed and leaned over to give Shirley a gentle kiss on the forehead. As she did, she took her guest's hand and pulled it to her chest, rubbing Shirley's hand over her bosom.

"I like that. You're beautiful, Shirley. Mind if I join you?"

Without waiting for a response, Sarah Ryan pulled away the covers and lay down next to her guest, her hands gently caressing Shirley's breast and her stomach, her naval, and finally between her legs where gentle massaging caused her to shiver once more. Her whole body tingled. It was the strangest Shirley had ever felt in her entire life, but she liked it. Whatever fears she may have had quickly disappeared as the two women found themselves in a tight embrace, holding, pawing, massaging and kissing each other. The two college students missed no parts in exploring each other's body.

Shirley Konowitz was awakened by the sound of dishes. She looked up to find her hostess in a pair of jeans and a sweatshirt making breakfast.

"Eats coming' up." What would ya like for breakfast, lady? Sarah's Diner ready to serve ya," she shouted, trying to imitate a New Yorker's accent to the delight of her guest.

"Back in a second." Want to use the bathroom. Got to wash up. "Don't have an extra toothbrush hanging around, do you?" Shirley asked.

"Look in the medicine cabinet. I usually keep a spare there. You never know when I'll have an overnight guest," Sarah shouted over the clanging of the dishes.

"Take your time. Coffee'll be up when you get out," she added.

The stream of hot water was wonderful. Not only did the shower wash away the perspiration and the sleep from the night before but it also stripped away any feelings of guilt that Shirley Konowitz may have felt from her first intimate experience with another woman. In fact, she hummed in the shower and smiled to herself as she lavished her entire body with the soap. Realizing she had left her clothes in the living room, Shirley carefully wrapped herself in a towel, her arms folded in front of her chest.

"I'd say you're modest. Whatcha think this is? A public restaurant? You don't have to hide your boobs from me. I've seen 'em before, Honey."

Sarah left the kitchen and walked to where Shirley was looking for her clothes.

After the guest had put on her panties and bra, Sarah reached out and gave her a big hug. As she did so, her hands reached for the bra straps and suddenly Shirley was bare from the waist up. She didn't know what to do. She stifled a shout as she felt her hostess' lips on her breast, licking her pink nipples, which had by now hardened. Within seconds she felt hands on her behind caressing her soft skin.

Shirley felt her knees buckle as she fell naked onto the sofabed. Her hostess was on top of her.

With one hand Sarah Ryan continued to caress her guest while with the other she expertly lifted her own sweatshirt to bare her breasts.

With her sweatshirt above her neck, Sarah quickly unbuttoned her jeans. Kicking off the Levis, she jumped alongside Shirley and together the two college students again found themselves in a deep and passionate embrace.

"I'm coming…I'm coming," shouted the hostess as she rubbed her body against Shirley's.

"Are you enjoying this? Are you coming?" she moaned.

Shirley was silent. She fearfully admitted to herself that she felt wonderful.

After what appeared to be an eternity, Sarah Ryan and Shirley Konowitz arose from the sofa bed and oblivious to their nakedness, walked into the kitchen where they poured coffee into two mugs, and brought their drinks into the living room.

"I think I should get dressed and leave. I feel funny sitting here without clothes on," Shirley whispered.

"Fine, Sweetheart. I'll just sit here and watch you get dressed," Sarah Ryan responded.

After Shirley had put on her clothes, she watched as Sarah put on hers. She found Sarah to be provocative as she slowly and deliberately stepped into her panties and snapped her bra, and put on her sweatshirt and jeans. When done, she walked into the bathroom, emerging moments later. She helped Shirley remove the crumpled sheets and fold the bed, and together they relaxed over coffee and toast. Sarah looked at her watch. It was close to eleven when she got up. She thanked Sarah and walked toward the apartment door.

"Hope we can do this again?" said Sarah Ryan as she kissed her guest on the lips.

"You're a great guest and you were really helpful last night. You know what I mean. I never could have gotten the dishes done without you. Will we see each other again?" Sarah asked.

"Of course. You're not so bad a hostess either," Shirley said as she winked. She closed the door behind her and walked down the flight of stairs to the street below. On her way back to the dorm, she whistled. She was elated and uncomfortable with her feelings.

Chapter 5

The medical examiner's preliminary report indicated that the woman had died from a compression of the neck. He confirmed that the initial examination showed no signs of a struggle and there were no signs of scratches on her body.

"Hell, New York brings people from all over the world, especially young people. We don't have a clue whether she was a native of this city, had come from Los Angeles or Chicago or Charlotte, or any one of the thousands of cities and towns making up the United States of America. We don't even know if she was American," Torre said when he called with the news.

The Park Police and NYPD were working together but also independently on the case so Torre and I were on the phone every day. By now the investigation was a full-time job and my commander gave incoming assignments to different lieutenants so that I could focus totally on this particular case. The personnel files told us nothing that would help in the investigation. However, they did raise some suspicions that required further review. During the next two weeks, therefore, the two of us scheduled interviews with the rangers. We thought it would be better to meet off the island at Torre's office in Lower Manhattan.

* * *

Leo Brandwyne Jr. hesitatingly asked for a glass of water and slowly nursed the drink as he held the white Styrofoam cup. He was slightly built and stood about five feet six inches tall. I estimated he weighed no more than one hundred forty pounds soaking wet. Tortoise shell eyeglasses with thick lenses rested securely on the bridge of his nose and his temples were hidden under a thick shock of uncombed dark brown hair. His short goatee was neatly trimmed but he needed a shave. His long sleeved maroon and white striped sport shirt, open at the collar, was neatly pressed and his tan chinos were clean. He wore a rust colored corduroy sport jacket with leather patches on each elbow and could have passed for an Ivy League professor except that he wore white sneakers instead of penny loafers.

Brandwyne sat quietly waiting for us to speak. He had put the cup on Torre's desk and his hands rested on his lap. He fidgeted and appeared nervous. He took off his glasses and with a tissue he removed from his pocket proceeded to wipe them.

"You ain't a suspect. You don't have to say nuttin' and if you want, you can have a lawyer present. This is standard procedure." Torre reached into a desk drawer and removed a small laminated card and read Brandwyne his Miranda rights. Brandwyne nodded his understanding.

"Just so you know where we're coming from, we had to read ya your rights. Again, you ain't a suspect," the detective continued. We asked the ranger about his career, why he joined the Park Service, and how he liked his job.

"Call me Skip, please. That's what everybody calls me. I hate the name Leo. I'll celebrate my fourth anniversary with the Park Service next month. The only reason I stayed so long has been to please my father and grandfather. I'm third generation Park Service but I hate it here and want out."

The ranger said he was born in Fayetteville, North Carolina where his father served with the 82nd Airborne Division as a paratrooper. His mother was a teller at a bank branch on the military post where she met her husband.

"My father received an honorable discharge and left the Army when I was nine. We drove to Arizona in our old Plymouth so that he could join the Park Service at Casa Grande National Monument in Coolidge. I'll never forget that car. How we made it out west beats me but we did. There was no heat or air conditioning and half the time the radio didn't work." Brandwyne smiled for the first time.

"My dad turned in his Army uniform for another. He's always worn a uniform. I don't recall ever seeing him wear anything else except an old pair of jeans and jersey at home or a pair of chinos, shirt, tie and jacket for when we went to church on Sunday mornings."

A partial smile again appeared on Brandwyne's face. I made a mental note of the reaction.

The ranger explained that because his family didn't stay in one park too long, neither they nor he developed permanent roots.

"I grew up in government housing complexes that were always the same mobile homes, small apartments and attached buildings. Anywhere my father's career took us. I've been to many parks in a lot of states. I can't begin to count them or remember half of them. All I recall from childhood is driving from one part of the country to the other until the old Plymouth died and we bought a used Pontiac station wagon with 85,000 miles on it."

Brandwyne said that he went to high school in Maine. His father had returned east as a ranger at Acadia National Park. When he graduated, he attended the State University but in his junior year his parents left for another park assignment. He stayed in Orono to complete his undergraduate education, finding an apartment and part-time jobs in the area. During the summer he worked as a deckhand on the Bar Harbor to Yarmouth ferry which pretty much covered his expenses.

"Being separated from my parents was the best thing that happened to me. My father can be a tyrant. Always wants to know where my mom is twenty-four hours a day. They don't have many friends. Says he has no use for any of them. Says they're all too liberal. You know. They support equal treatment for blacks and gays. Dad doesn't go for that. Maybe once in awhile they'll go to a local movie. That's about it for their social life."

"I guess your mother accepts that," I interjected.

"She really has little choice. Sometimes I wonder what she saw in my old man when she married him. He always checks the car odometer to make sure she hasn't driven too far. If she's a few minutes late coming home from the supermarket he has to know where she went and why she wasn't home on time. He has a little notebook to keep track of mileage and oil changes and expenses. Every time she comes home from the store he marks the mileage in his little book. He has a fit if she forgets to do it or returns the car with less than a half tank of gas."

I asked if his parents helped him pay for college.

"I didn't get much help from them. I guess mom would have sent me a check once in awhile except they didn't have much for themselves. While I was in school I wanted to go into business but my parents and grandparents persuaded me to enter the Park Service when I graduated. Carry on the family tradition. I really didn't want to. Just between you and me, I hate the uniform and what it stands for. I'd leave tomorrow if I had the guts to do so."

Brandwyne suddenly became more animated with enthusiasm. He told us his ambition was to own a restaurant or manage a hotel somewhere in an off-beaten town. He didn't care where it was.

"I don't have any roots so it doesn't really matter. I'm dying to wear a normal pair of slacks and sport shirt to work, even a tie if I have to, like to go to the weekly Rotary or Lions Club meetings."

Torre asked him why he didn't get up enough courage to leave. Brandwyne stared at the sergeant for several seconds and said nothing.

"You want to know why, sergeant? I'm intimidated by my old man."

"When was the last time you saw him or spoke to him?" I asked.

"I was home last Christmas and we had a nice visit. I left on a positive note and I told them I was looking forward to seeing them again. I think they appreciated that."

Didja discuss leavin' the Park Service?" Torre inquired.

"Yeah, it came up once. I let it casually slip into the conversation. You know, what do they call it? A trial balloon? I did mention it to my father."

"What was his reaction?" I asked.

"Dad was smoking a pipe. He was sitting in his favorite armchair. Mom was in the kitchen doing dishes. He put the pipe down and looked at me without saying anything. Dad then said that he would like me to carry on the tradition. The same bullshit he always told me. 'Do what you want. It's your life and you're a grown man, but you're our only son and we'd be mighty proud if you would stay in the system. I know your late grandfather would be mighty proud too.' Is that the classic guilt trip scenario? If my dad had a college degree he'd be dangerous." Brandwyne smiled again.

"Did he threaten to cut ya off from his will if you defied him?" Torre continued.

"Hell no. Nothing like that. You know, officer. His look, his comment. I felt like shit, excuse the expression. I think you know what I mean. I left home on a positive note overall, though. It was good getting away from New York for a few days and enjoying my mom's cooking. After the holidays, however, I felt depressed for several weeks because I really don't want to hurt my parents. They're really good folks. I'm confused and haven't made up my mind. I'm leaning towards resigning the Park Service. I've got to wait for the right moment." The young ranger looked at us both.

I asked him when that moment would be. He said he wasn't sure.

"Did your parents say anything else? What's your mother's reaction?"

"Frankly, Lieutenant Finnegan, I don't think she gives a damn one way or the other. She's always gone along with what my father wants in order to keep peace in the family. I think she's really scared of him. She's a good woman. She has her own problems. Down deep, though, I think she would support whatever decision I make. On the other hand, I'm out of the house and she has to live with my old man. There's no other family for her to reach out and talk to except for two sisters and their families. They're still back in North Carolina. She writes and talks to them. That's one of the few non-essential expenses she's allowed to incur. She's allowed to speak to them five minutes a week. Doesn't see them very much either. It costs too much to fly east."

"And your father?"

"As I said, my dad's a control freak. He's got this thing for uniforms. He grew up in the Park Service and the military. His father—my grandfather—was from out west and I think stayed at one park for his entire career. Things were different then, I was told. You know, loyalty. Why move around? Establish your roots and stay there. I'd bet my father never ventured more than twenty miles from home until the Army. Gramps never traveled like we did and he never gained a high pay grade. He loved his job as a maintenance man and laborer. My father never went to college either. He joined the Army out of high school and has been wearing a uniform ever since," he repeated.

I asked what he thought the worse reaction would be if he went against his father and left the Park Service.

"Oh I don't know. I guess he'd be pissed off for a while and threaten to cut me off from his will. I doubt he has very much anyway. You don't build up assets on government pay, living in government housing, and not being able to stake a claim to any substantial piece of earth to call your own. All you usually own is your car or pickup truck and whatever furnishings that are not assigned to you by the government. I don't even think he ever bought a pen or pencil. When I was in school I used the cheap government-issue ballpoints and yellow pencils. I think a lot of the kids in my classes did the same thing since their folks were government employees." Brandwyne chuckled.

"Getting back to your question. I think eventually Dad would get over the shock of not seeing me in a uniform. I guess I've got to get up enough nerve to make my own decision and do what's best for me."

"How did you get to the Statue of Liberty?" I asked Brandwyne.

"It looked like an ideal assignment that would give me a chance to meet people and see New York. I'd been to the city several times when I was in college and I loved it. I'd drive down with some college buddies for a weekend. We were younger then and had the energy to do crazy things like that. One of my friends had an old Chevy so we'd all pile in, share driving and expenses, and go nonstop until we hit Manhattan. When I heard about the opening at the Statue, I applied for it and got my law enforcement commission. Since I was undecided whether to stay or leave the Park Service, I felt, too, that working here had to help my advancement opportunities and my career. Talk to my dad, though, and he'll take credit for my coming here. He claims he pulled strings with friends in the Park Service in Washington to get me this plum assignment. Makes him feel important. But just between you and me, I really don't think he has any clout in Washington…Any more than I have, at least. And I've got zilch. I never mentioned on my application for the job that I was third generation Park Service. I wanted to do it on my own."

I asked Brandwyne about the other rangers

They're all right. I don't have too much interaction with any of them after work." He became animated when I asked about Gaines, Johnson and Miss Marcus.

Gaines is a pain in the ass. He hates people. He reminds me a lot of my father. Spit and polish. Rarely smiles. All business. If he was a lieutenant leading the troops into combat he'd be the first casualty. And not from enemy fire. Get my drift?" Brandwyne spoke kindly about Johnson.

"We like Johnson."

"Could he have committed murder?"

"Why are you asking me? Anyone of us could have done that woman in. Will does live on the island so he'd have access to the monument any time of day or night. And he's not one of us, if you know what I mean."

"Explain what you mean," I said. Brandwyne hesitated.

"Don't think I'm a bigot or anything like that. But Will is black and they have a reputation for liking women. I'm not accusing him of anything. But you asked me a question and I'm giving you an answer." Neither Torre nor I responded.

"You asked me about Jennifer. She's pretty and she lets everyone know it. She drives herself very hard and I hope she doesn't burn herself out. It would be shame to lose her."

"Why do you think Johnson asked her to open the monument?" I asked.

"Beats me. Maybe she was fooling around with Will and did him a favor. Maybe she didn't like his advances and he got even with her by sending her into the monument to find the body."

"You're speculating that they conspired to kill the woman or that one was getting even with the other."

"You can say that," Brandwyne answered.

"I trust very few people. Looks are deceiving. Look at my father. He'll charm your skin right off. But get him home and he's a totally different person. I'm not accusing anyone of murder. I am merely answering your questions forthrightly, gentlemen. That's what you want me to do. Isn't it?"

Brandwyne stood up and asked where the water cooler was located so he could refill his cup. When he returned I asked him about his childhood, whether he had many friends while growing up, and how the constant travel affected his social life.

"The whole Park Service is one large extended family. Everyone shares just about everything. Thanks to the federal telephone system, you have contact with all of your old friends anywhere from Orono to Omaha. Sometimes they even bed down with each other's husband or wife." He chuckled.

"We really thought nothing about leaving our new friends behind and moving on to newer friends. I call it the mating ritual." Brandwyne smiled.

I asked him to elaborate on bedding down. After an embarrassed pause, Brandwyne said that it usually happened in isolated parks.

"Everybody relies on neighbors for provisions, shopping, even encouragement and emotional support. There's really nothing to do at some parks. They're so damn remote you can't even get good TV reception. In winter the roads are bad and sometimes closed because of snowdrifts. In the summer the tourists crowd the good bars, restaurants and movie houses that sometimes are twenty miles away. And Hell, when a ranger's out in the field, sometimes for several days in isolated parks looking for a lost snowmobile or hiker, the kids are crying and the wife is lonely. She needs someone's shoulder to cry on or to help her overcome an emotional hurdle. I don't think anyone really gives a damn what happens," he said.

I asked Brandwyne if he knew of homosexual or lesbian relationships.

"It wouldn't surprise me. It wasn't that when my father worked for the service. At least that's what he told me. There was more respect. Who knows? Maybe some of the people I work with are queers. Christ. We've got everything today. Who ever heard of women law enforcement rangers? They're all over the place."

Torre asked Brandwyne to be more specific.

"Don't forget that some of the ranger housing is one small community. Even if they live in nearby towns. Young married couples often work as seasonals because they can't find permanent jobs. Maybe they work in different parks because they can't find jobs together. I know one couple, married three or four years, who work in parks fifty miles from each other. They meet on weekends and alternate driving to and from each other's apartment. Sometimes there's a chance for permanent hire or promotion for one so the other spouse stays behind until he or she finds something closer. It gets lonely without your wife or husband or significant other, especially if you're young. Does sexual orientation really matter? It's the friendship, closeness, and compassion. Who cares if your lover is of the same sex when you're lonely?"

I asked him if he dated much. I detected embarrassment on his face.

"I'm sorry you asked that question, Lieutenant Finnegan. I'm not comfortable with women outside the workstation. I…I…don't know how to react."

I asked Brandwyne how well he related to the women he worked with. The ranger answered that they all get along but added that when they were not in uniform and in civilian clothes the socialization was non-existent.

"We have an unwritten agreement not to butt into other people's lives. We get along fine and all of us would go to bat for the other. On the other hand, we try to separate our work lives from our social lives," he said.

Torre asked gently whether there was something in his childhood that caused him to be shy around women.

"I know it's personal and you don't have to answer if you don't want to," he assured the young ranger.

"I don't know. I…Well maybe it's just that I've seen too many relationships break up in disaster and lots of tears when one spouse or partner or friends move on. I want to wait until I'm established in a career. I want a job that'll last so that I'll be comfortable with a woman. I'm afraid that one of us'll get hurt if we get too close to each other emotionally at this stage of my life. Who knows where I'll be in two or three years if not sooner?" There was another pause. Brandwyne resumed his fidgeting and looked directly at the NYPD sergeant.

"I got another problem that no one knows about. You see, I was diagnosed several years ago with a rare disease. I'm a celiac. It doesn't allow me to eat many of the foods my contemporaries eat. How can I invite a date for pizza when I can't eat the damn stuff without getting sick? How can I take her out to a nice restaurant and bore her while I negotiate with a waiter over what I can and cannot eat and she feels guilty ordering right off the menu? I don't think you can understand this." Brandwyne shifted his attention from Torre to me.

"Sure, I can do things most normal people do. But what happens if she invites me to her apartment and says, 'let's call for a pizza or Chinese food or a deli sandwich? My disease isn't terminal and my doctor says I can lead a normal life and live with my problem as long as I don't walk in front of a moving truck, but I'm afraid a woman'll laugh at me if I can't go to a normal place to eat like she can. I'm afraid if we ever got serious she'd be scared that our kids will inherit my genes."

Torre responded.

"Don't answer if you are uncomfortable, but have you ever slept with a woman?"

Brandwyne's face turned crimson and he stared at his hands, which were tightly clenched around the arms of his wooden chair.

"I…I…I guess not," he said softly.

"That's OK. Nothing to be ashamed of," Torre responded. From the look on his face, I sensed that Vince was as embarrassed by the question as was the ranger.

Sensing Torre's predicament, Brandwyne spoke.

"Don't sweat the small, stuff, Sarge. Don't feel badly 'cause you put me on the spot. I wouldn't know what to do or how to go about it. I wish I had the nerve to approach a woman and ask her out for a date. But I don't want to be rebuked. Maybe that's why I'm afraid to go against my old man and quit this Goddamned job once and for all. I hate the bureaucracy and hypocrisy, but at least I've got security. They can't fire me. Maybe once I'm set in my career decision and settle down my social life'll change."

"When Miss Right comes along, you will know it," I assured him.

I then asked the ranger whether he had discussed his concerns with anyone.

"There must be appropriate support groups."

"Yeah, there are groups. I've gone to a few meetings in Manhattan and on Staten Island. Would you believe all they talk about is food and recipes? I went to one meeting where all they talked about for over an hour was bread machines. Can you see me sitting there listening to shit for an hour on how to bake bread? Unless you have the disease no one really listens. Besides, no one cares about my problems anyway. They're mine and I'm going to have to work them out and live with them one way or the other. Before I was diagnosed, a doctor wanted to send me to a psychiatrist. He thought my problems were in my head. Can you believe that?"

"Have you tried to discuss your concerns with the women you work with? Maybe they know some girlfriends who'd be patient with you and help you out of your dilemma."

"You mean help me with my food sensitivities or go to bed with me?"

"Someone who'll talk to you. Put you at ease. There must be women with their own hang-ups and problems and fears and who knows, maybe they're worse than yours are. You can't isolate yourself," I told him.

"Where could we talk? On Liberty Island? And where could we go? Can you imagine me and say Jennifer going for a burger and I'd sit there nursing a Pepsi? I don't think that would go over well with her."

I had the notion that there was more to this young man than we were getting to. Sure, he may have had a hang-up with sleeping or getting too involved with a woman based on his park experiences outside of New York, and I knew he wasn't pulling our leg about his food problems. But I thought he was playing it to the hilt to perhaps cover something up. I made a mental note to pursue this further.

I then asked him what, if anything he knew about the dead woman. He answered that he had some thoughts on the matter, which he did not wish to discuss.

"I already told everything I know to the officer who interviewed me after the body was found. All I'm going to say is what I said before about the morals of park rangers. Ninety-nine percent of the rangers are extremely dedicated, totally conscientious, and devoted to their husbands or wives and their children. On the other hand, some of the rangers here, like me, come from isolated parks so nothing would surprise or shock them. Beyond that, I won't comment on what may or may not have gone on here that night. I don't know, gentlemen, and frankly, I don't give a damn."

"Do you have any idea who she was or why she was here?" Torre asked.

"No. Only what I told your detective."

"Where are your parents now?" Torre asked.

Brandwyne said they were in Southern California. They had retired from the Park Service and were living in a mobile home park outside of San Diego.

"As I told you before, my parents live and die for the Park Service and idolize the uniform. They devoted their entire lives to the system and now they're trying to get by on my dad's relatively small pension. He gave the government the best twenty-five years of his life with dedicated service. All he's got to show for it is a couple of plaques that aren't worth the wood they're engraved on. I don't want that to happen to me," he said.

"Do you think you'll leave the service?" I repeated.

Brandwyne said eventually and that it was a good possibility.

"I already told you what I think. Look at the people I work with. My boss Gaines is a horse's rear end. He couldn't hold a job in the private sector for a week with his attitude and personality. But the higher-ups look the other way. They let him go on embarrassing his staff in front of the public and don't say anything. Is this the best they could do for site like this? And his deputy? Again. William is a really nice guy. But I understand he had some personal problems before he came here. Can't prove it. Nor do I care to. But again, everyone's talking and it isn't the way it should be."

I asked him to elaborate.

"Well. You know what I mean. That diversity crap. I won't go into it anymore."

"You feel the same about the two women you work with?"

"Yeah. I already told you my feelings about women carrying firearms. It just is not right. Suppose there was real trouble inside the monument. Like a hostage situation. Could they handle it? We'd have had worse trouble. And Jennifer thinks she's a hot ticket. She's got a great body and attractive face and she flaunts it."

"Has she ever come on to you?" I asked.

"No. Not directly. But she makes sure you know she's got good looks. I wouldn't be surprised if she was sleeping around with some of the other guys around here. But again I can't prove it."

When asked again how his mother and father would react if he left the Park Service, he reiterated that they'd probably be mad for awhile but would get over it.

"Is there anything else you'd like to tell us?" I asked him. He nodded negatively.

I gave him my business card and he was excused.

After he left, Torre expressed doubts about the young man's future career.

"That kid was pretty frank and open. But he knows more than he's telling us," Torre said, scratched his head.

"If that's the case, Vin, who in Hell is he protecting?"

Torre merely shrugged.

"Somehow, we're going to have to visit Liberty Island and talk to the superintendent. Perhaps he can shed some light on the after-hours activities and hang-ups of his staff." I said.

Chapter 6

I arranged to interview Phil Varga, the most senior of the ranger staff, and I got to Torre's office fifteen minutes early. A few minutes before ten, the desk sergeant called and told Torre there was someone to see us.

Varga knocked on the door. Without waiting to be invited in, he swaggered into the office. He immediately sat in one of the wooden chairs in front of Torre's desk and introduced himself.

"I know you're gonna ask the question anyway so let me put all my cards on the table from the start. I know I'm early for my appointment. Yes, I detest most women. I didn't kill that broad. Anything else?"

Varga was tall with a stocky build. He weighed more than two hundred pounds, most of it in his gut. His receding hairline, grayish blond hair and simple eyeglasses made him seem older than his 50 years. Despite his apparent assertiveness, neither Torre nor I could determine immediately what he was thinking or how he'd react to our questioning. I liked his straightforwardness, on the other hand.

His plaid shirt separated above a wide brass belt buckle, which bore a beer company logo, and his jeans appeared slept in. He wore cordovan cowboy boots. The ranger was neatly groomed and what hair he had left was combed. His legs were crossed and he held his right ankle with his left hand as he waited for our questioning.

"Shoot guys. What can I do for ya?" As he had done with Brandwyne, Torre read the Miranda rights from the laminated card and instructed the ranger that he didn't have to answer any questions and if he wanted one, he could have an attorney with him. I assured him that he was not a suspect and that this was part of the investigation.

I asked Varga to tell us about himself. He said he was born in Sieverville, Tennessee, just outside the Great Smoky Mountains. "I'm a real farm boy."

His father had bought an old log cabin and with a brother disassembled and carefully marked every log. After transporting it one hundred miles to where the family owned some property, the brothers reconstructed the cabin. They lived off the land and made a good living selling produce to local markets.

"I grew up near the Smokies and can probably tell you the name of every hill, trail and vista in the whole dang park. I love the outdoors. When I graduated from high school I joined the Park Service and I've been in the system ever since. I don't think I'd ever want to work in the Smokies, though, on accounta I probably know most of the people who grew up in the area or their children. I know too much about the area and its people."

I asked him to describe in general terms his career and what brought him to New York and to the Statue of Liberty.

"I've been in the Park Service for more than thirty years. Like I told y'all, it's been my whole life and I can't say it's treated me bad. Most of my assignments have been out west. You've probably already read my personnel records so there's no use in rehashing that bullshit. I planned to end my career in New Mexico to be near my daughter and her husband since I do miss the grandchildren. Dang if I can figure out a way on this Goddamned salary to fly out to see them very often." He then removed an old leather wallet from his back pocket and showed us a photograph of his family.

"These are the most precious things in my whole friggin' life. Don't ya ever forget it," he said.

"I'm hoping to get outta here one of these days and transfer back to a park in the Southwest so as to cut some of my movin' expenses when I do pack it in."

Torre asked when he planned to retire.

"Damned if I know, sergeant. I can't afford to live in New York and I can't afford to retire. Whatcha call that? The damned catch twenty-two?" A smile crossed his face.

Torre asked him to elaborate on his first statement about detesting most women and Varga's relaxed face tightened in anger. I noticed his fingers gripping his ankle as he weighed his response. After a pause of several seconds, Varga spoke and his face became flush. He admitted that his wife had run off with a younger and better-looking ranger whom she had met when they were in the Everglades.

"Who knows where she is today? I was out in the damned swamp up to my ass with the alligators workin' my back off and she was screwin' this guy while I was away. I was damned pissed but I got over it. It still hurts once in awhile, though."

Torre asked about his daughter. Varga said that she tried not to take sides.

"She never mentions my ex-wife when I speak with her. That's why Debbie and I get along just fine. In fact, when her kids call me gramps it melts me like butter."

Varga launched into a monologue about the Park Service and how it treats its employees unfairly. The damned bureaucracy looks out for its own. It doesn't really give a good Goddamn about the rangers who work their asses off to make this agency what it is. If I wasn't working so many friggin' hours away from home in the friggin' swamps, maybe I'd still have my wife and a decent home. You want to know why I came to New York? To get away from that shit. I ain't saving a fuckin' penny from my pay since it's so damn expensive to live here. At least I ain't in the swamps chasin' alligators and looking for lost hikers and shit like that."

"Can't you apply for a transfer back out west or south where the cost of living is cheaper? With your seniority you should have a good shot at it," I said.

"You know it's the same old horse manure. They all take care of their own. Once you leave the traditional regions out west or even down south, they forget about you. Unless there's someone in the regional office working for you, you're stuck here. When I came here I was promised a higher grade and that the urban experience would get me into a good position to move on. But once you're here they forget about you. Only a coupla years in New York and you'll move on. Shit I've been here five years and I ain't goin' nowhere. It's not that I ain't tryin'. I'm busting my stones applying for every job that I see advertised. But unless you're a minority or a woman or a lower grade or you got political or family clout you ain't goin' outta New York. Get your urban experience and you'll never be sorry. Shit. The lyin' bastards ain't kept their word about nothin' and I'm still here and I don't like New York. Nothin' personal gentlemen. Washington's given up on Phil Varga and shit, Phil Varga's given up on the system. That's as simple as that. I ain't lying to ya. But you can bet the dang mortgage that I ain't got anything to do with the broad that was killed. I don't even know who she was or what in Hell she was doing here that night."

Torre and I tried to digest what Varga had told us. Having been in the Park Service for so many years and seen so many other rangers come and languish in New York, I couldn't totally disagree with him. Then he continued.

"Between my rent for the one room apartment on Staten Island and my food bills, all I have left is change for an occasional beer with the guys. I guess you guys think all I do is drink beer," he said with a smile as he put his hands on his gut.

"But don't believe it."

"Tell us about the other rangers?" Torre asked.

"Not much," he said.

"I come to work nights so I won't have to stay alone at home watching TV and wondering what my ex-wife is doing with that guy she ran away with. Who knows if they're still screwin' around or ever married each other?"

"What was your assignment the night of the murder?" I asked.

He explained that as senior ranger, he generally took it on himself to supervise the younger staff.

"I'm comin' across as a hard-ass, but I'm really a good guy. I enjoy workin' with the young rangers and giving them pointers. CPR, first aid, handling crowds. They like to pick my brains and I like workin' with them. They're a good bunch of kids. And, of course, there's the usual paperwork. Reports and all that kind of stuff that keeps bureaucracies running. There's a report for this and a form for that. Would you believe there's even forms to requisition forms when you're out of them? What was I doin' that night? As I said, nothing unusual. We usually sit around in informal bull sessions and talk about techniques and procedures. I hope they learn from my experience. And we rotate patrolling the island and checking the monument." Varga stared at Torre and me for several seconds.

"We are isolated over there and so when we're actually walking around the island several times a night someone is always at the monitors. I don't want you to think we sit around and play gin rummy since we do work hard from the time we come on duty until the time we leave in the morning. It's not an easy job, believe me, gentlemen" Varga said.

He was asked again what his specific job was the night of the murder. He added that he took a turn inside the Statue around shortly after coming on duty with one of the other rangers. Everything seemed to be in order. He confirmed what Jennifer Marcus had told us earlier about the closed circuit TV.

"And nothin' outta the ordinary showed up on the monitor that you're aware of?" Torre asked.

"To the best of my knowledge everything was quiet and in order. Both on the monitors and during our physical inspections of the monument, sir," Varga responded.

"You said you don't have a clue about the identity of the dead woman or how or why she got there," I injected.

Varga's face reddened.

"Don't have any idea, Sarge. I'll say this. If she was here and shouldn't have been, damnit, maybe she got was coming to her. What person is dumb enough come to Liberty Island after hours? I wouldn't be a bit surprised if...No, I don't know who she was and why or how she got here," the ranger continued.

"What were you going to say?" I asked him.

"Nothin'. Oh nothin'. I was just thinking of something. I changed my mind. I think I'll keep my thoughts to myself," he answered.

"Have you complained to Washington about your problems? You know, low grade, cost of living, and desire to leave New York?" I asked him.

"Sure...I'm known as the pain in the ass of the Park Service. I'm always writing to the Office of Personnel Management with my gripes, filing grievances and calling our union representative. I even wrote to some Congressmen. You should see my stack of form letters in response. They all say they'll look into it. Nothing happens. That's another one of my gripes against women. Ya know this affirmative action shit puts us guys at a disadvantage. How does a fifty-year-old white guy buck the system?"

Torre, who had been taking notes, seemed oblivious to the previous conversation. He then put his pen down.

"How old is your daughter, Mr. Varga?" he asked.

Varga thought for a moment and responded that she was twenty-eight.

"About the age of some of the rangers ya work with, correct?" he asked.

"Yep. That's right."

"Do you guys work as a team?"

"Pretty much so. We stay together during our shifts. There' aren't too many who like working all night at an isolated place like the island so I guess you can say that," he added.

"Then ya know the rangers you work with pretty well."

"Yeah, I guess so. As good as anyone else, I guess."

"You said the rangers work as a team. Would you classify them as your surrogate children?"

"That's a good way of putting it. I never thought of it that way. They *are* about my daughter's age give or take a couple of years and I *am* old enough to be their father. Scare's the Hell outta ya, doesn't it?"

"Do you ever discuss personal problems?" the sergeant persisted.

"Like what?" Varga asked.

"Ya know, like father to son." Torre rested his right elbow on his desk, leaning over to get closer to the ranger. He stared for a moment at the wall behind Varga.

"D'ya think any of the rangers is capable of murder?"

"You mean could any of 'em be implicated in the woman's death?"

Varga stared back at the police sergeant as if in deep thought.

"Unlikely, sergeant."

"Possible?"

"Anything is possible. I don't have a degree in psychology so I can't pick their brains. But who would've thought my wife would've left me for a young dude? I didn't have a clue."

"Do you keep a log of activities on the island?" I asked.

"What do you mean?"

"An administrative record or diary where everyone signs in and out so you can keep track of where they are at all times."

"There's a notebook. We sign in and out. We all carry two-way radios so we're never outside of range. Besides, how can we go too far? Liberty Island is really small."

"Could a ranger sneak out for about a half hour or forty five minutes and not be missed? You aren't always together on patrol or in the same room at the same time. Is that correct?" I pursued.

"Yes. But it's highly unlikely."

Torre, who was listening intently, piped in.

"Tell us what you know about the rangers who live on Liberty Island, Mr. Varga."

"You mean the Park Service families. We don't have any married families. The last superintendent had a wife and three kids but when the children went off to college and it was he and the wife alone, she complained of getting stir crazy. So he put in for a transfer. They got outta there to a park in a different part of the country. But as I said, he had more political clout than I do. We just have single people living here and occupying the houses now. One building is like a dormitory. The others are single family units."

Torre asked Varga if it was possible that the dead woman was visiting one of the single rangers who live on the island.

"Could be. Who knows? On the other hand, this is an open place and it's impossible to hide anyone. Even if she *was* staying with one of the single guys. How would she get into the monument? The only keys to the building are kept in the office except for Johnson and that asshole, Gaines. They're the highest-ranking guys on the island. They keep a set of keys with them all the time. And there's maintenance. They keep extra keys in their office. I'm guessing their keys are all locked up when no one's around."

"You said that Johnson keeps a set of keys with him…"

"You're not thinkin' that Will coulda killed that woman, are ya? It isn't likely. William wouldn't hurt a fly. In fact, we kid him about finding a woman and settling down. Frankly, I think he's married to the Statue of Liberty."

"Ya said Gaines has a set of keys, too," Torre said.

"Probably."

"Where does he live?

"Somewhere in South Jersey. I don't know the name of the town."

"Did you see Mr. Johnson at all last night?" Torre continued.

Varga answered in the negative.

"Could Gaines have killed that woman?" I asked.

Varga stared at me.

"That miserable son of a bitch. I don't trust him. Let me take that back. He's got to be the meanest hombre in New York. I ain't got no use for him. None of us do either. If he walked in front of my car, I wouldn't step on the brakes. But I wouldn't go far as to call him a murderer."

"I didn't ask if he murdered that woman. I asked if he *could* have. There's a big difference," I said.

"Sure. He could have done it. But so could I have. If you put it that way, any of us could have done it. But I don't think so, Lieutenant Finnegan. You wanted my opinion. Now you've got it. That's not to say that he didn't do it. But I think it's unlikely."

"What about Johnson?" I continued.

Again Varga stared at me.

"Will is a decorated war hero. He was shot up pretty bad in Vietnam. He's a class guy. I'd be the first guy in line to be a character witness for him. Sure. He could have done it. But as I just said, any of us could have done in that woman. I'd find it hard to believe Johnson is implicated in any way. We were talking one day and he told me his story. He did have some problems many years ago, though. Who knows? Maybe he's back to doing the stuff. No. That ain't possible. But I sure won't put my money on it."

"I'm going to ask you a couple of personal questions, Mr. Varga. Don't feel ya have to answer them if you don't want to. You're not a suspect although we read ya your Miranda rights," Torre said.

"Don't sweat it. Shoot away and I won't answer if I'm uncomfortable, sergeant."

"D'ya date at all, Mr. Varga?"

"I said before I don't have extra money for that. I can just about afford a few beers. B'sides, I'm still getting over losing my wife. The only woman I care about is my daughter. Can't trust any of 'em as far as I'm concerned."

"Did you say how much longer you expect to stay in the Park Service?"

"Maybe about six months. Maybe a month or two more or less. If this case ain't solved by then, I'll probably have to stay around longer. I guess I am a suspect," he said, looking at both of us.

"To tell ya the truth I'd love to get out of here sooner than that but it depends on several factors including like I said earlier. I don't have any money to move or retire and I can't get a transfer back out west so I can cut my moving expenses when I do pack it in."

"Anything else?"

"Personal issues I'd rather not discuss if you don't mind," the ranger answered.

"Let me reiterate what ya said earlier. The woman coulda visited one of the residents who live here. You don't account for the whereabouts of every ranger every minute they're on duty. Is that correct?" Torre asked.

Varga stared at the detective.

"We have a log. We don't check every minute, though. If you're trying to get me to implicate another ranger, I'm not going to do it. In answer to your questions, in general terms yes on both counts."

There were no other questions and Varga was dismissed. Torre scribbled some notes on his pad as the ranger closed the door behind him.

"Two possible suspects. Both have a grudge against the Park Service. One's got hang-ups against women," Torre reiterated to himself.

""If you want my opinion, I don't think either of them had anything to do with the dead woman," I said.

"Never rule out anything or anyone, Mike."

CHAPTER 7

Shirley Konowitz wasn't happy with her career. She dreaded the thought of listening to other people's problems. She hedged between finding a job in a school system or in private practice, however, and did not seriously pursue her career search.

She moved to New York City after graduating from college and found life in Greenwich Village much to her liking, fairly carefree, and full of fun. She frequented the old coffeehouses, adored the college atmosphere of Washington Square, and during the day she waited on tables in a small cafe. At night she always found someone to talk to or go to a movie with. Her mother back home had settled down to the life of a single woman and adjusted to the divorce.

She, on the other hand, was unsure about her sexuality. After her experience in Sarah Ryan's apartment, she enjoyed one-night stands with women as well as men. She never exhibited outward lesbian tendencies although her experiences with women left her much more fulfilled than she ever felt having a man. She nonetheless enjoyed male company. It was relaxing to chat or even sleep with anyone who was willing to be her partner. Consequently, she always had someone to share her bed.

Shirley did develop an attachment to a would-be actor who had come to Manhattan from New Hampshire to pursue a career. On weekends when both weren't working, they generally traveled uptown to Central Park, the Forty-second Street Library, or to museums where they walked hand-in-hand and occasionally took in a movie in one of the local cinemas. She continued to play the field although Jim was the only true friend in her life.

The young woman awakened early one Sunday morning in February in a depressed state. There was little to eat in the refrigerator and she was short of cash, having gone overboard on her last paycheck to buy some much-needed clothes. After staring at the ceiling from her bed, she walked to the bathroom, showered, threw a terry robe over her naked body and boiled some water in the tiny kitchen so that she could make a cup of coffee. Putting a slice of week-old rye bread into the old toaster her mother had given her when she left Boston, she sat at the table reading Saturday's newspaper. Her hand was resting on her lap and unconsciously she moved her fingers up her leg, under the fold of the robe and rubbed herself where Jim had been only a few nights before. The sensation felt good so she continued to stimulate herself. The whistling of the old kettle on the gas stove did not disturb the young woman enough to interrupt her pleasure. Having finally reached a climax, she stopped and walked to the stove and turned off the burner. The hot steam coming from the small spout of the kettle felt good as it blew toward what was now her open robe. Instead of pouring the hot water into her cup, she returned to her bed where she threw off her robe, separated her legs, and engaged in a more premeditated and relaxed self-fulfillment.

Even the ringing of the telephone near the kitchen table didn't deter her… After eight rings the phone was silent, but Shirley Konowitz was totally oblivious. Finally she stopped. She again walked into the small bathroom where she took another shower, lathering her entire body and feeling sensual.

"What am I doing," she said to herself as the water from the tap sprayed over her entire body. She scrubbed her entire body, making certain, however, that her fingers did not go near the part of her body that had aroused her earlier. She shut the tap, walked to the closet where she found a pair of old jeans and a sweatshirt, and left her apartment, making sure to lock the door behind her.

Walking along lower Broadway with no specific destination, she took time to browse in some of the old clothing shops and at the headlines on the front pages of the local tabloids stacked in the yellow, green, red and blue vending machines along the sidewalk. She then instinctively entered one of the small cafes where she generally knew most of the customers and staff.

"How ya doin' Shirl? Haven't seen you in awhile. Everythin' OK?" shouted the counterman.

"Yeah, Charley, I've been busy looking for work," she responded.

"Any luck?"

"Not really. No one wants to hire me. Can't find a thing. Guess I'll have to stick with my waitressing. Pour me some brew will you?" she said as she grabbed a Danish from a tray under a large plastic cover on the counter in front of her.

"Oh damn it. Must have left my money in the apartment. Can you trust me 'til tomorrow, Charley? Promise I'll pay up."

Shirley grabbed a newspaper from the counter, walked with it under her arm, the pastry in one hand and the coffee mug in the other, to a table at a far end of the small cafe.

Should look at the ads. Maybe there'll be a job, she thought as she settled down to relax and enjoy her late breakfast. As she turned the page to the classified section, another customer placed five dollars onto the counter and spoke quietly to the counterman.

"This'll cover her tab and mine. Keep the change." The stranger walked to an unoccupied table and sat down to nurse a second cup of coffee and a chocolate donut.

This stranger found her fascinating. Thoughts raced through the stranger's mind about what kind of body lay underneath the lose sweatshirt and whether or not the buns under the jeans were as firm and taut as they looked from a couple of tables away. No words were passed between the two. One was intent on glancing at the woman with the newspaper while the object of attention sat totally oblivious to the benefactor who had paid for her breakfast.

Shirley looked at her watch. The old Timex read 11:55. She grabbed the paper and brought it back to the counter along with her dirty coffee mug and dish and told Charley she'd see him the following morning to straighten out her bill. Charley was too busy to respond. He never got a chance to tell her someone he'd only seen casually in the coffee shop previously paid the bill in full.

When Shirley Konowitz left the coffee shop, the stranger also got up and walked to the door.

Chapter 8

Our impatience was growing and we weren't alone. I got a call about a month after we started the investigation from the superintendent of Liberty Island.

"Michael, Sam Belmont. The higher-ups are coming down hard on me. They want some answers. The bureaucratic game. Regional office pressured by Washington who's pressured by some Congressman who got some nasty letters from constituents. I need some answers and I need them fast."

Belmont asked for a meeting. I agreed to meet the following morning at eleven.

"Heaven only knows. I am aware that you are working hard. I know you have the odds stacked against you. But I plead with you to apprehend a suspect. As I told you, Michael, I am being pressured from several sources. Just this morning I received an inquiry from the Secretary of Interior." He removed from his pocket a handwritten letter he had received.

Dear Mr. Superintendent:

My name is Jessica and I am nine years sold. My grandparents are planning to take me to New York City for my birthday and I am looking forward to coming to your city. I have never been there before.

The only problem is that I am dying to visit the Statue of Liberty but my grandparents don't want to take me there. They say the island is unsafe for children my age. My mom and dad agree with them and I am desperate. I don't want to come to New York City if I can't visit your statue.

Is there anything you can do to persuade my parents and grandparents that the Statue of Liberty is safe for nine year old girls like me?

I will be eternally grateful if you could write them and persuade them to take me to see the Statue. If you do, you will be my friend forever.

Thank you.

Their names are Mr. and Mrs. Lindsey Scott, 12436 Minnesota Avenue, Chicago, Illinois, 60607.

Jessica Scott.

"This is one of the better letters. You should see the mail that is sitting on my desk. They've been critical of the way we have been dragging our feet. I've got stacks of memos to return calls to Congressmen. Every day I get large envelopes from the Secretary of Interior's office, the Park Service Director's and Regional Director's offices with stacks of letters, cards and e-mail messages about this murder. My bosses and the Congressmen will not accept anything short of resolution," Belmont said.

"You must solve this case as quickly as possible. Is there any information you are able to share with me? Any glimmer of hope? Anything at all you may tell me in the strictest of confidence?"

I stared at the superintendent for several seconds.

"I understand your concerns. I want to close it too. I haven't slept a night since the body was found and my wife is ready to divorce me over the time I'm spending, even when I'm home. That's all I talk about.

She's afraid my ulcer will act up. Trust me. I will bring it to closure. Now while I'm here, do you mind if I ask you a few questions?"

Sam Belmont nodded in the affirmative. The tall gray-haired superintendent sat erect in a wooden armchair. His tan slacks held a crisp crease. His beige shirt and brown tie matched his dark brown sports jacket. Belmont's face and actions, however, reflected his nervousness. He frequently crossed and uncrossed his legs. He fidgeted with a pen that he repeatedly removed and replaced in his shirt pocket during the dialogue.

"How much do you know about your staff? Do you have any ideas about who brought the woman to Liberty Island?" I asked.

Belmont sat quietly. His right hand moved through his full head of hair as he pondered the question. He could provide no insightful details.

"What about Gaines? He stormed into the room like gangbusters and raised holy Hell with us," I said.

Belmont remained silent for what seemed to be several minutes. In reality it was only a couple of seconds. I know since I watched the second hand on the clock that hung on a wall behind him.

"Bringing Ron to Liberty Island as chief ranger was one of the few mistakes I have made in my Park Service career. He had an excellent record before coming east. I needed someone to restore discipline among the rangers. I'm embarrassed to admit that he isn't what I expected. He's a dangerous individual. Too damn absorbed with his own importance. I wish I could get rid of him. Until and unless he violates regulations or leaves voluntarily, there is nothing we can do with him. The regional director and I discuss the situation frequently. We have made repeated efforts to relocate him. He is a hard man to move because of his reputation throughout the system. No other superintendent wants him. It's that simple. If we could find a superintendent willing to take him, we could order a direct transfer; a lateral move without his permission. The problem is his attitude. On the other hand, although his personality leaves much to be desired, his record is clean…It's as shiny as his cordovans which I assume you've noticed are spit and polish."

I smiled.

I then asked him about Johnson. The superintendent had nothing but praise for the deputy.

"Really hard worker. Dedicated member of the team. One of the finest men you can find anywhere. I wish I could take credit but I can't. Bringing him here was not my decision. I want you to know that. We were told the regional office wanted him and I had no say in the matter whatsoever. I thought that this was just, how should I say it tactfully, one more chance to fulfill our affirmative action goals. But we were all pleasantly surprised and thrilled to have William with us. He won't have a problem should he wish to move on which we hope he won't do for some time," Belmont continued.

I asked whether it was possible that either Gaines or Johnson could be implicated with or have known the woman who was murdered.

"Unlikely. Totally unlikely. Johnson loves this island. He would not do anything to tarnish it or the image of the Statue of Liberty. As for Ron Gaines? As you know, he's been a pain in the backside, a hard-nosed individual who is too impressed with this position to do anything as stupid as become implicated with a woman on Liberty Island. As for both gentlemen, I'm afraid I cannot help you."

I asked about Jennifer Marcus. Belmont said she scored high with the public and there were no complaints filed against her but that he found her to be a confused and misguided young woman.

"She comes from a broken home and looks to older men as a father figure. I trust that some of this may change with maturity. She's a delight to have as an employee. Never given any of us a bit of trouble. On the other hand, as I said moments ago, we receive many complimentary calls about her."

"Ms Marcus appeared to be in total control of her emotions despite the fact that she discovered the body," I said.

The superintendent said he was not shocked.

"Jennifer Marcus is a competent ranger. She can be in total control of her emotions. I think she needs to control her desire to please men when she is off the island, gentlemen."

"Have you had any social encounters with her?" I asked.

"I take insult to that question, Michael. I will not respond to that inference. A person of my rank and age who is happily married to a wonderful woman neither needs nor desires the company or sexual favors of a young lady. Especially one with whom I interact on a professional level. The issue is closed."

"What about Phil Varga?"

"Why can't he get a hardship transfer out of New York? He's desperate to leave."

Again the superintendent blamed it on the bureaucracy, claiming he was doing what he could to accommodate him.

"There are no openings for him at the present time. Phil likes working with the young men and women and he is a fine role model for them. I hope you are not considering him as a suspect. He would be the last person in the world I would suspect. Besides, he is so much older than the dead woman. He tends to growl and complain. Down deep he's a pussy cat."

"Age don't mean a damn thing, Sam and you know it," I said.

"If there are no more questions, Michael, may I take leave? Before I go, again let me impress upon you the need for expedience in resolving this horrid crime. We must find the perpetrator as quickly as possible. As long as the case remains unsolved, my career and that of other dedicated men and women in the Park Service, including Mr. Varga who you asked about are in jeopardy. Do I make myself clear?"

CHAPTER 9

Sam Belmont was becoming concerned about William Johnson. He had heard various rumors that the deputy chief ranger had recently been acting strangely. He started to show up for work late and rarely left his office except for lunch. His office door was usually locked and he didn't communicate with his staff unless it was necessary. Belmont called Ron Gaines into his office when a memo over the deputy ranger's signature crossed his desk.

"Are you aware of this, Ron?" Belmont asked as he handed over the memo. The memo read:

> *Effective this date and until further notice, the Statue of Liberty will be inspected between seven-thirty and eight o'clock each morning by a member of the ranger staff on a rotating schedule. Any matters requiring immediate attention will be directed immediately to the appropriate administrative, law enforcement, or maintenance supervisor. All staff will be required to take the early staff boat to the island on their assigned duty date. There will be no exceptions. Switching of inspection dates will require approval of the deputy chief ranger in advance.*
>
> *Signed William Johnson*

Attached to the memo was a two-month schedule.

"Yes. Will and I talked about it. He's been very stressed out since the murder. Wants out of the early morning inspections. I sense he's putting himself under a lot more pressure than he deserves. I told him I have no problem with this. In fact, I encouraged him to go ahead with the idea. Those bastards on the night shift do nothing but goof off when Will and I aren't around. It's about time he gave them more responsibility. If I lived closer to the island, I'd sneak back from time-to-time to keep them on their toes. But Will's too nice a guy," Gaines said.

"Is there any other reason? We're all under stress. This is a drastic departure," Belmont said.

"If I can speak confidentially, Sam." I hope Will's not reverting to his previous problem."

"Drugs? He's been dry for many years."

"I didn't say that, Sam. I meant that he's in a constant state of depression and I hope that it doesn't lead to more serious consequences. He and I are like brothers. I don't want to see Will get hurt or hurt himself."

Belmont questioned whether he could believe what he was hearing.

"Have you and Will discussed this?" Belmont's elbows rested on his desk as he twisted a pen between his fingers.

"I've tried. He won't talk about it. Lorelei's called to invite him over for dinner and spend the night. He loves our kids." Gaines lied. He never discussed Will with his wife.

"What was his response?" Belmont asked.

"He declined. Said he didn't want to impose."

"Have you two discussed Will's depression?"

"He said he didn't want to talk about it. It was his issue and he'd deal with it on his own."

"What else did he say?"

"He claimed that the ongoing investigation and suspicions of him were getting him down. He claims he's a prime suspect and that he's afraid he'll go to jail for being an accessory to a felony but that he's innocent." Gaines lied again.

Belmont picked up the phone and dialed his secretary. He asked her to arrange an appointment for that afternoon with the deputy chief ranger. The superintendent noticed that Gaines was sweating.

"How are the rangers responding to this memo?" he asked.

"They don't like it. They've gotten so dependent on Will Johnson opening the monument every morning. This puts added pressure on them to meet the boat and do some work early in the morning. This upsets their routines. But I think it goes deeper than that, Sam. One or two of them have told me they're afraid this is only the beginning. They're afraid Will will do something drastic." Gaines again misled his boss. His eyes avoided the superintendent's. He fidgeted with his hands.

"How are the staff reacting?"

"They all know about Will's past problems. It's no secret. They're afraid he'll…"

"Use drugs again?" Belmont interrupted.

Ganes continued to avoid Belmont's stare. He nodded affirmatively. He felt he was walking into a trap. He had to divert the superintendent's focus to a safer issue in which he didn't have to cover up his repeated lies.

"You know, Sam. This rotating schedule really isn't a bad idea. It gives the rangers a chance to handle new assignments. From a professional perspective it also relieves one person from all the pressure. I got the impression that Will was getting tired of the same daily routine. He probably would have instituted this new duty roster anyway."

Belmont remained silent. He knew that Gaines was lying. How could he prove it? More importantly, *what* or *who* was Gaines hiding? Why was he implicating his loyal assistant?

* * *

Belmont sat on one of the upholstered office chairs next to his deputy chief ranger.

"What have you heard about the investigation?" he asked matter-of-factly.

"Nothing, That's why I thought you called me. I expected to see Ron here, too."

"How are you holding up under the pressure, Will?"

"I'll never forgive myself for sending Jennifer into the monument that morning. I get the feeling that the police think I put her up to it to cover something I was involved in. It's becoming difficult to do my job here. Did you ever get the feeling that people are subconsciously second-guessing your decisions? I've tried to mingle less with the troops until this is all over. Maybe when the case is resolved it'll be better for me to move on. It might be best for everyone concerned. That's unless I go to jail."

"Don't be silly. I will have no part of that. You did what you thought you had to do. Isn't everyone entitled to deviate from his daily routine once in awhile?"

"Tell that to Lieutenant Finnegan and Sergeant Torre. I'll bet they're preparing their indictment papers at this very minute."

"Cut the nonsense Will. You know that's not true."

"What makes you think that? Do you know something that I don't?" Belmont seemed puzzled.

"Can't you see it, Sam? I'm single. I was fooling around with a woman and planned the perfect crime to cover up a tryst inside the monument. I knew all the angles and areas where the monitors couldn't catch us and when we had an argument I killed her. Then I ask another woman to find the body. I can see the prosecutor telling the jury about my violent temper and my former drug habit. Of course, being African-American adds to the picture. Black man finds white woman. Black man kills white woman. Black man deserves life in jail with no parole. And then my liberal white attorney from the ACLU defends his African-American client by blaming it on the white man's war and on society. You know. The white man's war fought by black men." Johnson began to laugh.

"I assume, William, that this is a fantasy and not a confession." Johnson became silent.

"Why'd you ask me here?" the deputy chief ranger asked.

"Something else is bothering you. What is it?"

"I don't know what you're talking about, Sam."

"Look. You come into the office later than usual. You remain in your office and you don't mingle with the rangers as you used to do. And this memo." Belmont pulled the memo from his shirt pocket and handed it to Johnson.

"I can't sleep. I'm up most of the night. I'm deathly afraid of what the police are thinking. I usually doze off in early morning and sleep through the alarm. My appetite is gone and I've lost about ten pounds. But I've not had a drink, popped any pills, or shot my self up. You've got to believe me."

"I do," Belmont whispered. He desperately wanted to believe the young man seated next to him.

"You think I'm back on drugs."

"What makes you think that?"

"I don't know. Intuition? Gut feeling?"

"I must tell you, William, that I am deeply concerned about you. I don't want to see you get hurt. You have come a long way and you have a long and great career ahead of you. Don't screw it up. I'm talking as your boss and as a friend. Trust me."

"Yes sir," Johnson said softly.

"Are you and Gaines still on friendly terms?"

"Yeah. We argue occasionally about Vietnam. But yes, we're friendly. I've not been to their home in awhile. I miss their children."

"Why haven't you gone there?"

"I don't go where I'm not invited. I guess if Ron or his wife called, I'd take them up on their invitation. But I don't like to barge in on anyone. They've got their own lives." The deputy chief ranger pondered the last question.

"Have you and Gaines spoken about me?"

"Why do you ask?"

"What did he tell you about me? Did he say that he invited me but I refused to go to his home?"

"Why would your good friend do that?"

"That's what I'd like to know. Did that bastard make up stories about me?" Belmont remained silent.

"Your not answering me gave me the answer I was waiting to hear."

Belmont walked to a small refrigerator behind his desk. He removed two cans of ginger ale and brought one to his deputy chief ranger.

"Ya know, Sam. When I came home from Vietnam I swore I never wanted to see another dead body. I feel now as I did when I was hospitalized. No appetite. Don't want to talk to anyone. Just leave me alone." Johnson popped open the can and put the can to his slips.

"I still smell the stench of corpses, and the cries of grown men wake me up in the middle of the night. And seeing the body of that woman in the monument. It reminded me of Vietnam. I've been fighting the demons inside me since then and I'm afraid I'm fighting a losing battle, Sam." Johnson carefully placed the can on the carpet next to his leg. He covered his eyes with his big black hands and began to sob.

"That bastard ran away from the war. Now he's screwing me. Why in Hell doesn't he leave me alone? It's bad that he jumps over everybody else. I thought I was his good friend," Johnson muttered.

Belmont rose and put his arms on Johnson's shoulder.

"It must have been tough. You're a brave man, William. Yes. You are a very brave soul. God bless you."

Johnson regained his composure. He stared at the superintendent.

"Yes. I believe you. I truly believe you, William. My heart goes out to you. I've made up my mind. I'm placing you on 30-day administrative leave with pay. But you must get some professional counseling. Call the employee assistance coordinator. We need you around here. I've got some big plans for you. But you must exorcise those demons. I know you'll do it."

Johnson relaxed. He thanked Belmont.

"I really didn't have anything to do with that murder."

"I know," Belmont responded.

Chapter 10

I arranged to meet Miguel Garcia at Torre's office. He arrived fifteen minutes late.

"Terrible what happened to that woman," the ranger said in broken English after apologizing for his tardiness.

Seeing the cigarettes on Torre's desk, he asked if he could smoke. Garcia removed a filtered cigarette from the pack in the pocket of his flannel shirt.

As he had done with Phil Varga and Skip Brandwyne, Torre read Garcia his Miranda rights, assured him that he was not a suspect, and asked the ranger to describe what he was doing the night of the murder.

Garcia's right hand moved to his head and pushed back his dark black hair. His elbows rested on the arms of the chair. He stared at the smoke of his cigarette before answering. He outlined how he walked around the island, returned to the law enforcement office where he cleaned his pistol, polished his shoes and did some general housekeeping. He also took his turn at the dispatch desk.

I asked if he saw anything suspicious on the TV monitors.

"You mean did anything grab my attention, lieutenant?"

I nodded.

"Nada. I didn't see anything. I swear."

I asked how often he checked the monitor. He said every chance he got.

"What types of things do you read?" I asked.

"Everything I can. I want to improve my, how do you say it, command of the English language."

He explained his plans to go to college and earn a bachelor's degree. He extended his arms upward and his palms faced the ceiling.

"But that ees is out of the question right now. I do not have the money or the time." he said.

Glancing at his wedding band, I asked him about his wife and how she liked his working nights.

"She goes to law school. She wants to be an immigration attorney to work with people who want to come and stay in America. Maybe when she's earning some money I will be able to go to college."

Garcia explained that his family had come to Florida from Cuba when he was a young man and that most of his family still lived in the Miami area. He came north in hopes of finding a better way of life, staying with an elderly aunt and her husband in the Bronx while he completed public school.

Torre noted that Garcia's English was quite good. Garcia admitted he spoke two languages, English and Spanish. He was the only member of his family except his wife to do so.

"I am very proud to be an American citizen. I love this country and would do nothing to hurt it."

As we talked, I noticed Garcia's clothes. His slacks were pressed. He wore a sport jacket over his flannel shirt. He seemed relaxed and comfortable in our presence and spoke lovingly about his family in Miami. But he expressed doubts about his career.

"Rosa wants me to leave the Park Service. She wants me to earn mucho dinero. Real money, you know?" Garcia's ears reddened.

I asked him again about his home life.

"That, senor, ees one of my problems. My wife, she ees much

unhappy. She wants me at home with her but she's always so busy studying. When I'm home we don't talk much on account of she's into her books. So what's the use?" Garcia shrugged his shoulders and raised his arms skyward.

""How d'ya deal with that?" Torre asked.

"With much difficulty, sergeant. She also thinks I am a flirt. You know making eyes at other women. She doesn't like that. I've got Latin blood. That's the way it ees. She doesn't understand. You know what I mean?" A smile crossed his face. The young ranger realized the implications of Torre's question and his response.

"Occasionally I, how do you say it, stray? Fool around? But I'm' a man and I'm entitled, Si? I like a fling once in awhile. But that's only when my wife is visiting her parents or something like that. Can you blame me for liking women?" He fingered the wedding band while he spoke.

"I would really not do anything to hurt my wife. I love her very, very much and I think she loves me, too."

I took a liking to the young man.

Torre than asked him what he knew of the two women who worked with him on the night shift. He said they all got along fine.

"Do they ever join you and the others for a drink after you get off duty or for coffee on your way home in the morning?"

Garcia said that they occasionally stopped for breakfast on leaving the Park Service boat.

"If any of the women or the other men knew the dead woman, d'ya think you'd know about it, Mr. Garcia?" Torre asked.

"It's hard to say. We talk about our lives, especially at night when everything is quiet. Sometimes we discuss personal things."

"D'ya ever discuss your frustration because your wife is always studying but she wants you at home with her?"

"What do you mean, sergeant?"

"Do the women ever come on to you?"

"Make a pass at me?"

"Yes."

"Oh no, Senior. I make certain that I do not mix business with pleasure."

"Do you ever see William Johnson when you're on duty?" Torre asked.

Garcia explained that he saw Johnson rarely. Only on those occasions when the deputy chief ranger passed the administration office on his way from the Park Service boat to his apartment.

"Does Johnson ever entertain guests at his apartment after hours?" Torre continued.

Garcia smiled but didn't answer.

"You mean a señorita?"

"Yeah."

"Nada. Will isn't the type. He doesn't date much. He usually stays by himself. He's very serious. He's a very good man and I like working for him."

"Do people who visit the other residents ever sleep over?"

"Not too often. There's no way to get back to Manhattan until the first ferry leaves at 9:45. By that time it's too late for the guests to go to work. Only Park Service people and guests on official business are allowed to use our boat."

"If a woman visited a ranger on the island, say for dinner or drinks, you told us there'd be no way for her to get home until the morning. Is that correct, Mr. Garcia?" Torre asked.

"Si Senior."

Torre lifted a pencil from his desk and twirled it between his fingers.

"D'ya love your wife, Mr. Garcia?"

"Si, senor, Very much. Mucho. I already told you that."

"Does she love you?"

"Except when we argue about my career and the fact that she spends so much time over her books."

"How much longer does she have to study for her degree?"

"Another year. I think. Then who knows how much longer she will have to study for her bar examinations. Then she has to find a job."

"Then what will you do?" I asked.

The ranger pondered the question.

"To tell you the truth, Senor, I do not know. If Rosa gets a good job I will leave here and try to go to college myself."

"Will your wife be as supportive of you as your are of her?" I asked him.

Garcia smiled. He looked at me.

"Only if I cross my heart and promise her I will stop flirting," he said.

We asked him about another dozen questions and I was satisfied that he had been honest with us. He then left after shaking our hands and thanking us for being patient with him.

During the next few weeks we interviewed the remaining rangers. One, a woman from the Midwest, admitted she was angry with men in general because of her father. A successful physician in Minnesota, he inhibited her mother, her sister and herself with his domineering qualities. She did admit, however, that she had a boyfriend, a rock musician, and that they hoped to become engaged within the year and eventually marry.

What struck me as odd was that she couldn't wait to introduce her fiancée-to-be to her dad.

"I'd love to see the expression on my old man's face when he sees Brad. Brad's long hair and earrings will knock dad's jock off."

I was about to eliminate her as a suspect. Then Vince Torre asked her if she thought a woman could have been responsible for the death. Without saying a word, the ranger got up and left the room, closing the door behind her.

The other ranger, Paul Chadwick, was a gregarious young man whose full head of blond hair immediately caught my attention. The Connecticut native who lived in New Jersey said he worked his way through a state college and was accepted into Rutgers University for a master's degree in education. He took a summer job with the Park Service in order to earn some money but liked it so much he gave up his graduate work to apply for a full time position.

"I thought the Park Service offered me a chance to utilize my history and education background and let me work in a safe environment. Talk about safe environment. Damn. We've got a dead woman on our hands. That isn't too safe, is it?"

Chadwick told us he married his high school sweetheart. They had grown apart and eventually divorced and she moved out west. His wife was the only child of a successful accountant and he couldn't live up to her financial standards and needs. Her parents had spoiled her rotten. He claimed to have not been aware of it until after they married.

"Her poor father. He was a really cool guy and I liked him a lot. But the poor bastard's going to have to work until he drops to support his wife's and daughter's shopping and spending habits," Chadwick said matter-of-factly.

We asked him about his social life. Although he admitted to dating occasionally, he said he really wasn't into the social scene. When we asked if he had any idea who the dead woman was or how she got to the Statue of Liberty, he responded negatively. According to my notes, he did comment that people do things for strange reasons and that he wouldn't doubt that the woman knew someone on the staff.

"You don't need a Ph.D. from Harvard or Yale to figure it out. How could she hide out in the Statue of Liberty? How'd she know where to hide without being spotted by our rangers or the cameras inside the monument? And how did she get there in the first place? Certainly it takes smarts to be able to hide out after the last visitor leaves and suddenly appear in the early morning without anyone knowing you were there for twelve hours. Unless, of course, someone hid you where he or she knew you wouldn't be discovered," Chadwick said.

For some reason, Torre pursued Chadwick's social life. The ranger admitted he had two special girlfriends, both of whom he was intimate with at fairly regular intervals.

"I was screwed by one woman and I don't intend to let it happen again by marrying."

When asked how he related to the two women with whom he worked on a regular basis, he said they were colleagues. Socializing beyond the job never entered his mind.

"We're all professionals and act that way toward each other."

Torre also pursued Chadwick's comments about whether he knew who the woman was. According to my notes, I sensed that he had become nervous and edgy and although he wanted to say something, remained silent on the issue.

When he left, Chadwick asked us for business cards in case he wanted to call us.

We agreed that Chadwick would provide additional information.

"We gotta be patient, Michael," Torre said in a fatherly way as he put his arm on my shoulder.

Chapter 11

It was one of those frightfully hot July evenings. Jennifer Marcus was alone in her apartment. She spent the early part of the evening writing letters to her mother and to some college friends. Since her apartment had only one window air conditioner, she grabbed a light sweater, locked the door from the outside, and left to walk around the neighborhood.

Her first stop was a small dimly lit coffee shop. After making small talk with the clerk behind the counter, she bought a pastry and coffee and carried the items to a small table in a far corner of the room that offered a good view of the room. No one she knew was around. She was alone but really didn't mind. She was certain she wouldn't be bored although at the moment there was no one to talk to.

An attractive young woman entered the cafe. Jennifer hadn't seen or met her. But something about her looked appealing and interesting. She watched as the newcomer jauntily strolled to the counter, took a cup of coffee and pastry and a newspaper and settled at a table not far from where she sat.

Jennifer got up and walked casually to the counter. She motioned to the clerk.

"Do you know her?" she whispered as her head momentarily turned toward the stranger.

"Yeah. Comes in quite a bit. Usually short of cash. She's never stiffed us for a nickel, though. Why d'ya wanna know?"

"Just asking."

"Why?"

"Tell her the bill's taken care of," Jennifer said as she slipped the clerk a five-dollar bill.

"I can't do that."

"Listen to me. Small favor. Please?" Jennifer whispered.

"Well okay. But don't tell anyone. Just between the two of us," Charley said.

"Don't worry about it," Jennifer Marcus purred as she leaned over the counter. The loose fitting blouse attracted Charley's eyes.

Jennifer noticed the clerk began to blush. She leaned over further and whispered into his ear.

"There's more of this for you if you play your cards right. Do we have a deal?"

"Y...Yes..." Charley stammered. Charley continued to stare at the tops of her breasts. Her cleavage became more visible when she casually unbuttoned the third button on her blouse. Jennifer Marcus sensed he was trying to figure out whether she referred to the view he was enjoying or the money, or both.

Jennifer smiled broadly. She thanked the clerk and walked to a table near Shirley Konowitz. She removed a paperback novel from her handbag and pretended to read it while enjoying her snack. Her attention, however, was focused on the woman at the nearby table, the unsuspecting customer for whom Jennifer had paid the bill.

Suddenly the stranger walked to the counter, dropped off her dirty dishes, and left the restaurant. Jennifer got up too. She also made her way back to the counter. Her hands played with the buttons of her blouse, giving Charley another sneak preview of what he hoped would be the featured attraction. She shoved two one-dollar bills into his hand, winked, and left the restaurant.

Shirley was oblivious to the woman who followed her at a discreet distance. She stopped to peer at the used clothing through store windows along Barrow Street. She then browsed at the secondhand bookstore and casually walked back to her brownstone apartment. As she entered her building, Jennifer removed a matchbook and pencil from her pocketbook and wrote down the address.

Jennifer Marcus returned to the coffeehouse several nights later and again spotted the woman she had followed home. She put her fingers to her lips and looked at Charley while she nonchalantly played with the button of her blouse. She walked to the same table she had sat at earlier and nursed her coffee and muffin. She felt her heart beating rapidly as she eyed the young woman sitting a few tables away. As before, the object of her attention remained oblivious to her presence.

After about fifteen minutes, Jennifer approached Shirley Konowitz's table.

"Mind if I join you? Haven't seen you around here. My name's Jennifer…You can call me Jen. It's tough being a single woman in Manhattan on a Saturday night," she said matter-of-factly.

Shirley looked up in surprise.

"Sure. Grab a chair. Can I buy you some coffee?"

"Why not?" Jennifer responded with a smile.

Shirley walked to the counter and held up two fingers. Within seconds she had two steaming cups of coffee and was back to the table where Jennifer waited.

"New in town?" Jennifer asked.

"No. I've been here a couple of years. Live not far from here. I'm from Boston. Can't find a steady job I like. I do odd jobs waitressing until something interesting comes along. What about yourself?" Shirley asked.

The two women hit it off quite well.

"Want to hear something really funny, Jen? A few weeks ago I was sitting here and I was a little short of cash. When I went to pay the bill the clerk told me that someone had already paid for my coffee. Can you imagine that? In New York City someone I don't even know covered my tab. I'm still in shock. When you go out of town all people talk about is the cold people in New York. But I'm convinced that isn't the case. You ever have an experience like that?"

Jennifer acted surprised.

"Come to think of it, no. No one has ever paid for my meal except when I've been on dates, of course. But I was on the subway several months ago and asked for directions. Would you believe six people on the car took maps from their briefcases and helped me? It's a crazy world."

"Where do you live?" Marcus asked.

Shirley gave her the address of her brownstone.

"Would you believe what a small world this is? We live near each other. I guess we'll have to become friends. Have you ever been to the Statue of Liberty?" she asked.

"I can't say I have. I'd love to go some day."

Taking a pencil from her handbag, Jennifer wrote her phone number on a paper napkin and told Shirley to call her so they could get together.

After chatting for about a half-hour, Shirley got up to leave the coffeehouse. She liked Jennifer Marcus and looked forward to meeting again.

"Are you busy? Why don't you join me? I'm going back to my apartment." She and Jennifer Marcus left the restaurant together. Charley stood behind the counter and scratched his head. He was confused.

When Shirley Konowitz and Jennifer Marcus arrived at Shirley's brownstone, she invited Jennifer up to see her apartment. She accepted the offer and before they realized it the clock on Shirley's wall showed that it was one in the morning.

"Care to stay over? It is kind of late and I don't like walking alone at this hour so I'd feel better if you stayed until morning. What time to you have to be at work?" Shirley asked.

Jennifer explained that she had the day off and was relieved that she could sleep over. She didn't admit that she, too, was scared to walk the streets of Greenwich Village alone at this hour.

Shirley slept restlessly. She remembered her encounter with Sarah Ryan when she was in college. She was up early and without waking her guest, she showered, dressed and put up a pot of coffee. Jennifer got up about an hour later and the two young women continued to chat until late morning when Jennifer left.

"What say I call you on Wednesday or Thursday? Maybe we can get together at my place for the weekend," Jennifer said.

"Sounds great. I'll look forward to it. Have a great week," Shirley said as Jennifer Marcus closed the door behind her.

* * *

Jennifer Marcus was born in an Atlanta suburb. The corporation her father worked for transferred him to Alabama when she was in her pre-teens. He was rarely home after the relocation. His work as a sales executive for an international corporation took him all over the country. Her parents divorced amicably when she was in high school. Her mother hired a full-time housekeeper who Jennifer adored.

Her father's support payments were always on time. Although she was very close to her mother, she communicated with her dad and he never forgot important occasions. For birthdays or other milestones, he always sent a beautiful card with a generous check.

Mrs. Marcus did not remarry and maintained an active social life. She dated occasionally, was active in the Junior League, and her photograph was often in the newspapers for her voluntary activities within the community. She was also a doting mother, concerned about every aspect of her children's' lives.

When the University of Alabama accepted Jennifer, her mother made certain that her dormitory room was nicely decorated and that she had sufficient spending money. If Jennifer did not call home every Friday night, her mother called her. Both of her parents were in the bleachers watching her receive her college diploma. After the ceremony, her father accompanied Jennifer, her mother, and her siblings to dinner at a fancy restaurant.

Social life on campus had been average. Jennifer dated frequently. However, she did not care for the men in her drama and theater classes, calling them too fruity. She was closer to her sorority sisters. She feared marriage since she did not want to experience having to raise children in a fatherless environment as her mother did.

Chapter 12

I had become frustrated and impatient by our lack of progress. As a result, I was no longer even-tempered. I needed to either solve this case or take a long leave of absence. One morning after my wife admonished me to calm down, I called a staff meeting so that each investigating team could bring us up-to-date on their end of the investigation. I was going over some of my notes from that meeting when the phone rang. It was Sergeant Torre. We agreed to meet for lunch the following afternoon in Manhattan.

Torre was already there by the time I arrived at the deli on Broadway and Chamber's Street... He waved his arm and I joined him at a small round table in the back of the room. My friend appeared to be more agitated than usual, like he had some deep secret he had to get off his chest. He removed a package of chewing gum from his jacket pocket and slowly opened the outer wrapper, rolled the foil into a little ball, tossing it toward but missing the ashtray on the table in front of him.

"Ever get a hunch, Mike?"

"Yeah, sometimes. Most of the time they don't work out."

"What would you say if I told ya I thought the dead woman was invited to the island by someone who lived or worked there?"

"That's obvious. You're not telling me something we already assume," I responded. We had some leads but none of them panned out. Tips called in by strangers were not convincing enough to warrant further investigation. I was ready to listen to any new theory, even an old one if I thought it would help. Maybe it was time to focus on it.

"She was about the same age as the rangers with the exception of Mr. Varga. That makes me think there was hanky panky. Screwin' around or somethin' like that," Torre said.

The detective stopped talking when the waitress brought our sandwiches. He then continued.

"Strictly speculation. Remember the meetings with the staff the morning we found the corpse. Who found the body?"

"A young woman…Jennifer Marcus," I said.

"What was your first reaction when you saw her besides the fact that she was a good looker? Why didn't Johnson do the night rounds? Right? Too much coincidence, if you ask me."

"You're not saying there was a conspiracy between the deputy ranger and the Marcus woman, are you?"

"What I am saying," Torre continued, "is that Miss Marcus was pretty cool considering the circumstances. She's fairly new on the job, a young woman. Shit, Mike, I'd be scared out of my cotton pickin' mind if I found a body. And I've been a cop for more years than I want to acknowledge. What I am saying is that Miss Marcus was too much in control…"

I had thought of that theory but I didn't want to buy into it.

"Maybe your friend, that Johnson guy, could be a prime suspect despite what you think about him, Mike."

"Why do you say that?"

"Assigning the woman ranger to do what he usually did on the day a dead body was found is hard to justify. It's too much of a coincidence. Maybe they *are* working together and covering each other's ass."

I reiterated my doubts about Jennifer Marcus. I refused to consider William Johnson a suspect.

"I'd bet the mortgage against that one," I said.

"I got a gut feeling you'd better call off the bet or find a good apartment," Torre responded.

I opened my briefcase and removed the medical examiner's report that I was carrying around since receiving it.

"Did you read the report thoroughly?" Torre asked.

"Yeah. There were no signs of violence, no bruises and Ms X's body was clean as a baby's tusch. But she's dead and lying in the city morgue."

"Do you share my feeling that if it wasn't Ms Marcus and Will Johnson it coulda been one of the other rangers?"

"Anything is possible."

"I don't like Johnson's boss either. I got a hunch that he's more involved than he wants us to know. Maybe his coming on like gangbusters was a cover-up."

Torre urged me to look over my notes from our initial meeting at Liberty Island and our follow-up one-to-one interviews with the staff. Torre recounted the many circumstances that could lead to any one of the rangers, not just Jennifer Marcus and Will Johnson.

"There's that guy who hates the National Park Service. The third generation crap. He doesn't want to follow his father's footsteps but doesn't know how to tell his old man. He was very shy and didn't even walk into the room until we invited him in. Maybe he thought he could screw a broad inside the Statue where no one could see him. Besides, he wouldn't have to buy her a meal and watch her eat while he sat there feeling like a loser. He should know how to bypass the cameras since he's worked on the island for awhile. Suspect numero uno. Besides, nothing like a murder or rape inside the Statue of Liberty to shake up the Park Service establishment that he's got a grudge against," Torre said.

Torre continued to stare at me. Although the waitress had brought our sandwiches, he didn't touch his.

The sergeant then continued.

"Then there's that Varga guy, the ranger who's old enough to be the father of them all. He hates women. He could have vented his pent-up feelings by harming the woman."

I then recounted what we knew about Garcia and Chadwicke who both seemed likable but could not be ruled out as suspects.

Torre suddenly became animated and recalled our interview with the other woman ranger. He recounted how when we asked her if a woman could have contributed to the death, she stalked from the room without warning.

I suggested another meeting with Sam Belmont. We spent the next half-hour enjoying our lunch. I then called the superintendent…

"Oh yes, Michael, how are you? Haven't spoken to you in several days. Did they tell you that I had my secretary call on several occasions to inquire about the status of the investigation? I hope we weren't a bother to you."

I assured Belmont that I had received the messages but that I had been too busy working on the case.

"Besides, I have nothing new to tell you, unfortunately, Sam." I briefly summarized the medical examiner's report. The superintendent invited us to his office the following afternoon. "The press and the regional office are getting to him. He's starting to feel the pressure but I think he'll work with us. He wants this resolved so as he can wind down his career without a blemish. He wants to retire without this hanging over his head," I told the detective when I picked him up in front of his office. As we drove to the dock where a Park Service boat was waiting for us, the detective sergeant reviewed his notes in his leather-covered notebook.

"Medical examiner can't find any bruises or signs of foul play. No scratches, finger marks or anything like that. Nothin.' She died of suffocation and asphyxiation and the friggin' monument is air-conditioned. How do you figure, Mike?" he asked.

"Maybe she was hiding in a place inside the monument where there was no air conditioning."

Chapter 13

Jennifer Marcus stood on the deck waiting for the ferry packed with visitors. As the ferry glided smoothly toward the island, she tried to gauge the number of people on board. Looks like a full house, she said to herself. She walked to the ranger kiosk and grabbed the public address system's microphone.

Welcome to Liberty Island. Be alert to the health hazards. There are long lines to enter the monument and a wait of ninety minutes to climb the three hundred and fifty-four steps to the crown. Persons with heart problems or other health-related concerns are strongly urged to not attempt the climb. We encourage you to visit the gift shop and food area on your right as you walk toward the flagpole. You also are urged to visit the interesting exhibits within the monument. Ferries return to Liberty State Park in Jersey City and to Manhattan at twenty-minute intervals. The last ferries will depart at six forty-five this afternoon. Thank you and enjoy your stay with us.

No matter how hard she tried, Jennifer Marcus could not erase from her mind the memory of seeing the body lying on the carpeted exhibit area only a few weeks before. She kept asking herself how she managed to keep so cool. Did anyone really suspect her? Was she too calm during the interviews? Maybe I didn't do enough crying. But, she thought,

Will Johnson could vouch for the fact that she was spaced-out when he first saw her sitting on the floor inside the monument. I wasn't acting that time. I was really scared.

Jennifer couldn't get a rise out of Johnson and Gaines about what was going on and the police hadn't spoken to her since the initial interview. As a result, she was antsy. Whenever she passed the chief ranger and the deputy, she felt isolated. They seemed to ignore her. They never brought up the subject. Whether they discussed it behind her back or just thought her guilty never surfaced. No one said a word to her. This is what bothered her the most.

Her mother called just about every night to see how she was holding up. As the young ranger stood in the kiosk, she rehashed their conversation the night before in which her mother told her that several friends called to convey sympathy.

"You know my friend Marilyn. I play bridge with her every Thursday night. She called just a few hours ago and urged me to encourage you to come home for a vacation. Take your mind off the situation. That was very nice of her, wasn't it dear?"

"Yes mom, but I can't get away now. The police don't want any of the staff to leave the New York area until they apprehend the perpetrator. Only for an emergency. I have a responsibility and there's no way I can come home."

"Can't you tell then that this is an emergency? Tell them that your mental health is at stake. I'm certain the nice gentlemen will understand. Would it help if I asked our family physician to write a note to your boss? I'm certain that under the circumstances your boss and the police will let you leave."

"Mom. Don't you dare. There is nothing wrong with me. They won't let me leave New York and I don't want to run away. I am a big girl now. Don't you understand I'm a grown woman, a college graduate, and a professional with a law enforcement commission? Besides. I have my own life to lead."

"But Jennifer. I am your mother and I am concerned about your welfare. Some day when you have children of your own, you will realize what I am trying to do for you. Let me call Dr…"

"Don't you dare. If you do, don't ever expect me to speak to you again. Is that understood?" Jennifer slammed the receiver back onto its cradle.

After the last passenger departed the ferry and the visitors returning to New York boarded the vessel, Jennifer Marcus walked to the administrative office and knocked on the office door.

"Come in," Gaines shouted.

"Hi Ron. Busy?"

"No."

"Can I talk to you for a moment?"

"What's your duty station? Do we need relief?" Gaines was businesslike. He kept his eyes on the pile of papers in front of him.

"Station two, the dock. But the ferry just left. I've got twenty minutes."

"What's on your mind?"

"Mind if I sit down?"

"Pull up a chair. Excuse the mess," Gaines put down his pencil and quickly straightened the papers he was working on as if hiding them from her inspection.

"I'm scared, Ron," Jennifer blurted.

The chief ranger stared at her. He removed his glasses and wiped them with a tissue he pulled from a box in the top drawer of his desk.

"Ron, I don't know what to do."-

"Someone bothering you? What's the problem?"

"Can you keep a secret? You're the only one I feel I can confide in," she whispered.

Gaines felt himself flush in embarrassment. No one talked to him that way in his office.

"What's on your mind, Jen?" he asked sympathetically.

You know Goddamned well, what the problem is. Do I have to elaborate and spell it out? Ever since I stumbled on the body I've felt I'm under suspicion of murder. But there's more to it than being considered a prime suspect."

"Whoa. Slow down. You're not the prime suspect. No one has indicted or accused you. Get this straight. We're all suspects right now. You're no different than any of us. You've got to calm down. Don't panic."

"No Ron. Listen to me. I'm serious. I've lost my ability to function. Maybe I should ask for a leave of absence until this mess is resolved. I'm nervous...And...And...And I just don't know what to do. I can't explain it now. Maybe someday when this is over I'll tell you what I'm really worried about. But not now. I need time to think."

Gaines stood up and walked over to the young ranger's chair. He wanted to put his arm on her shoulder to calm her down but stopped short of doing so. He wanted to help her. But his office wasn't the place. Perhaps later when they were off the island. He feared that to touch her in her current state of mind, no matter how innocent the gesture was wrong. He fought the compelling urge to take her into his arms. He walked back to his desk and remained standing behind his chair.

"Why're you more scared now than before?"

"I feel the entire staff thinks I'm guilty, including the police. Why do you think I asked for the transfer back to the day shift? So I didn't have to face Phil and Skip and the others. Do you realize what it was like coming to work every night and thinking that they think I'm guilty?" She suddenly broke out into uncontrollable tears and asked for a tissue. She grabbed a bunch from the box Gaines' handed to her and began to wipe her eyes and cheeks.

"That just is not true. No one suspects you of anything. Get it out of your head that we're all talking about you."

He picked up the phone and dialed the dispatch desk.

"Have someone relieve Jennifer Marcus at station two for the next incoming ferry. She's not feeling too well and she's resting in my office. Have the deputy find a replacement for her on the next shift. She'll be alright in about an hour," he shouted into the phone.

The young woman remained seated and continued to wipe her face.

"What else's bothering you? You said you had something else on your mind and you couldn't talk to me about it now. Be up front with me. I can't help you unless you come clean," he told her.

"Please Ron. Don't push me. When I'm ready I'll explain. Right now I've got to get my head in order. I just want to think. Can I put in a leave slip for the rest of the day?"

Gaines tore a sheet from the pad he removed from his desk drawer and handed her one. When it was completed he initialed it and put it into an interoffice envelope for the personnel office.

"Go home and rest. And if you feel comfortable talking to me about whatever else is on your mind, call me and we'll chat." He got up and against his better judgment walked to her chair and placed a hand gently on her shoulder.

"Relax. Everything'll be just fine."

He left her alone as he stepped into the hallway. He walked toward the Statue of Liberty to supervise crowd control and handle other routine law enforcement matters. He suddenly broke into a sweat.

"Those bastards. I'll get those bastards yet. I'm not through with them," he muttered.

CHAPTER 14

At my wife's urging, I took the following weekend off and we spent the day at the beach. It was my first weekend away from the office since the fatal discovery and I needed a change, even if only two days. We relaxed and did nothing. A few neighbors invited us to a backyard cookout Sunday night so we returned home early, showered and changed. After a few beers, the guys pressed me for information about the murder. Even the women wanted to know if we had identified the body.

Of course, I couldn't comment on an ongoing investigation. I said we were hopeful of solving the case soon although we didn't have a clue or a suspect. We were groping for answers, hoping that somebody would come through with some fresh ideas.

I was well rested when I got to work Monday morning. Torre called at nine o'clock.

"Michael."

"When you call me that I know I'm in trouble. What's up?"

"I got another idea. I'd like to come back to the monument and look around the area where the body was found."

"Anything specifically in mind?"

"Now I got another hunch. Remember when we was lookin' through the items that were found on the island and inside the monument?"

"Nothing of any significance that I can recall."

"Forget the ordinary stuff. D'ya remember that one of the detectives found a screw?"

"Could've dropped from someone's pocket. Looked like an ordinary household screw from a light fixture or some other household appliance. Could even have held a house number onto the outside wall," I said.

"I don't know. That's what I gotta find out. Can you set up a meeting for one night this week after the last ferry leaves? Maybe around six?"

"Who do you want there?" I asked.

"You and me and the superintendent and a couple of your officers. I'll bring a few detectives." I also suggested Gaines and Johnson.

I said I didn't totally understand the significance of the screw Torre referred to. Torre admitted it could be a wild goose chase.

"It may be too far off the wall but I got some ideas I wanna try on for size. We'll talk about it when I see you. Any night this week'll be fine. The sooner the better. I wanna get this off my chest," he said.

I waited until after nine and called Sam Belmont. I anticipated what he would ask me and told him we were working on the case diligently.

"That's why I'm calling. Sergeant Torre and I would like to schedule another meeting after all the visitors leave. We *may* have come up with new evidence." I emphasized *may* to avoid raising Sam's hope prematurely. I told the superintendent to say nothing to anyone except Johnson and Gaines who were to be at the meeting.

"How many maintenance staff are in the monument at that hour?"

"Not many, perhaps three or four."

"Arrange for them to be away from the monument for about an hour. It is important that only you, Gaines and Johnson are there. Oh yes, we will have some of our detectives with us," I said.

"How many of you will be coming ? Do you want me to arrange for our boat to meet you at the dock in Manhattan?"

I said that a Park Service vessel would be fine since we wanted to avoid the chance of media monitoring the NYPD radio frequency.

"Did you say that you would like me to attend your…hmm…visit, Michael?" Belmont asked.

We agreed on Thursday night at six-thirty.

* * *

The Park Service vessel was at the dock when we parked our vehicles. We left Manhattan promptly at six thirty, arriving at Liberty Island about twelve minutes later. We retraced Jennifer Marcus' steps. No one said anything until we climbed to the second floor.

"Let me assure you that we will try not to take too much of your time. I know this is off hours but there are some questions that have to be answered. I know you have a two-hour drive back to New Jersey and that this has been a long day. The sergeant and I appreciate your patience, Ron," I said.

Gaines looked at me and I could read his mind:

"Why is that son of a bitch suddenly so considerate of my feelings? Only a few weeks ago his sidekick was kicking my ass. I don't trust either of them."

I ignored Gaines' stares and turned the meeting over to Torre. I noticed that Gaines appeared nervous for no particular reason. He shifted from one leg to the other. His arms remained tightly clutched around his chest.

Torre asked Johnson to recount again what happened when the body was found. The deputy chief ranger began to outline the circumstances for the umpteenth time.

"We've gone over this how many times?" Johnson seemed impatient.

He repeated what he previously told us and pointed to a specific spot on the carpeting where the body had been found.

"I believe we've already gone over all of this. Why do we have to rehash old information? I thought you had some new evidence. I'd appreciate it if you would get on with whatever you have to tell us, gentlemen. The medical examiner ruled out foul play," Gaines interrupted. His arms remained crossed in front of his chest.

"Thank you, Mr. Gaines. We will take that under advisement," Torre answered sarcastically.

"Please continue, Mr. Johnson," Torre said.

"Any idea how the body could've gotten here?" he asked.

"If I may interject, sergeant, Mr. Gaines is correct. We have already discussed this many times. We would appreciate your getting to the point and telling us about the new evidence you are supposed to have." It was the first time since the investigation got underway that I detected irritation on the part of Sam Belmont.

"Is this why you called us here at six-thirty at night? To rediscuss questions we already answered? I think you can do better than that," the superintendent added. I thought I detected a smile on the chief ranger's face. The first since we arrived on the island.

"Please be patient, Mr. Belmont. We're *all* under a lot of pressure. But keep in mind we have a corpse lying on a cold slab in a refrigerator in Manhattan and no answers as to how she got there and why. Sergeant Torre and I aren't here to waste your time," I countered.

"Thank you Michael," Torre said.

"And yes, Mr. Belmont and Mr. Gaines, I ain't in any mood to waste your time or mine either. But I gotta ask these questions for a reason you'll see in a minute. Please be patient." I knew he was putting on an act for Sam Belmont and trying his damndest to keep cool.

"Again, Mr. Johnson. Any idea why the young woman was here for Ms Marcus to discover?" Torre continued.

Silence.

"Is the torch accessible to the public?" the sergeant asked.

This caught everyone, including me by surprise. The superintendent responded that the torch had been closed since 1916 because of structural weaknesses and that the only access is by authorized staff who check the lighting and clean the torch at regular intervals.

"How often does someone go into the torch?" Torre pressed on.

Belmont looked at Gaines who uncrossed his arms from in front of his chest.

"Maybe twice a week. More frequently when we don't have heavy visitation during the summer. This time of year when the crowds are the heaviest, we press all our people into more important maintenance activities such as cleaning the rest of the monument and the grounds," he said.

"How many are authorized to go into the arm and the torch?" Torre asked. He stared directly at Gaines.

"There's one person in particular whose responsibility it is to clean the arm and the torch. Two others do it when he's off the island."

"Who are they? What are their names and job functions?" Torre pressed.

Gaines identified the regular torch cleaner and the two maintenance men.

"Who's this guy? The regular torch cleaner? D'ya think we oughta talk to him?" Torre asked.

"I doubt it. He's the maintenance man who usually leaves the island early in the afternoon since he's on the first boat over to the island in the morning," Gaines said.

"Any women have access to the arm and the torch?" Torre asked.

"Why do you ask?" Gaines responded.

"Just answer the question."

"Occasionally we use women on special duty or detail when someone is on vacation or out sick. They do the job in addition to their regular responsibilities. We found this works out fine. They take pride in what they do. In fact, they feel important and good about contributing to the overall operation," Gaines said convincingly.

"Let me remind you, Sergeant Torre, that all of our staff, whether they're maintenance or rangers, are efficient and highly motivated. We hire people who do take pride in their work," the superintendent interrupted.

"Would any of the rangers on duty the morning after the homicide have had access to the torch the night before?" Torre asked.

"Unlikely," Gaines said. It's only accessed by maintenance people."

"Has anyone ever entered the torch without the knowledge of the supervisor? Could anyone, say Lieutenant Finnegan, or me enter the arm without a maintenance person being around? Is the hatchway or entrance or whatever else you call it locked so that a special tool is needed to unlock it?"

Gaines responded that no special tools are necessary but that during the day there is adequate security to prevent anyone from opening the hatchway.

I asked if there was ever any breech of security. Gaines mentioned several instances but that in each case the perpetrators were apprehended.

"Where's the hatchway?" the sergeant asked.

Gaines pointed to a set of stairs.

We climbed to the third level where the chief ranger retrieved a stepladder from a cubicle behind a display case and he proceeded to climb it. He used a blade from his pen knife to loosen the screws that held the hatchway in place Torre asked to see the screws. He then handed them to another detective.

"Anything different about them?" he asked.

"Yeah, Sarge, one of 'em doesn't match the others. These screws look like they're brass. The one I found near the body is an ordinary household screw," he said holding up the one Torre had removed from the evidence envelope.

At Torre's request, the detective handed Gaines the screw that was found near the body and asked Gaines to tighten into the hatchway door hold. After some hesitation, the chief ranger inserted it into the socket and began to screw it into place.

The sergeant asked Gaines to remove the screw. Gaines handed it back to the sergeant. Torre turned to Sam Belmont.

"Superintendent Belmont. Can you tell if there's any difference between the four screws?" He handed Belmont the three screws that held the hatchway cover and the one he had retrieved from the evidence envelope. Belmont merely scratched his head.

"By golly. They are identical except for the color of one of them. At least they appear to be," he said.

Gaines, who remained on the ladder, began to perspire once again. No one else was sweating.

"Mr. Gaines. Is it uncommon to have unmatched screws holding the hatchway cover in place?" Torre asked.

"Screws are always coming loose on railings, exhibits and throughout the building. We keep a supply of all types of screws, nails, brads and other hardware for emergency or necessary repairs. Our staff may have seen a brass screw missing and figuring that no one would notice, replaced it with one from stock. Maybe the only screws in stock were the batch he took the unmatched screw from."

Torre stared at the ranger. "How often didja say your staff cleans the torch?"

Gaines repeated a few times a week.

"This isn't a common area. Only a few, I think ya said three people, have access to the arm. How can you account for the fact that a screw would become loose and drop from the hatchway if no one goes up there, except your own staff by your own admission?" he asked, staring into Gaines' eyes.

"Maybe it wasn't tightened securely when it was replaced and could've fallen out of the socket...Maybe...I don't know...I can't think of any other explanation. Our maintenance staff is very thorough."

"Are you implying, Sergeant Torre, that perhaps there was some sort of scheme between a member of our staff and that woman? Could it be possible that the screw you are producing is not from the hatchway but could have come from another source? It appears to be a fairly common item. It could be purchased anywhere...At any Home Depot or neighborhood hardware store. I am sure you will find a similar item in many fixtures in homes or offices. Why are you so certain that this is the same screw that was replaced here?" Belmont interjected.

"That's what we're trying to determine Sam," I said.

Torre turned to one of the detectives who had accompanied us. He asked him where he found the screw that he held in his hand.

"Near the body, sergeant," the officer answered. He pointed to the steps leading to the second landing.

"Now. One more time. Can someone kindly explain to me and Lieutenant Finnegan how the screw that Officer Rabinowitz found matches the other screws holding the hatchway lid? If it was an identical screw in terms of size, how was it lying on the carpet?" Torre asked.

His question was greeted by silence.

"Let's assume it came loose and fell to the ground or landed on someone's shoe or in someone's blouse or shirt collar. Or better yet, it was unscrewed from its socket by an unidentified individual and carried in his hand until it dropped to the ground," Torre mumbled as he paced the area.

"Why in Heaven's name would someone remove a screw and carry it with him? It has no material value. As I said moments ago, it can be purchased at any hardware store. And it certainly has no souvenir significance. I just do not understand your reasoning or line of thinking, I'm sorry, Sergeant Torre," Belmont shouted.

Torre stared at the superintendent.

"In other words, Mr. Belmont, you're saying that this damn screw accidentally came out of the socket, landed on the ground, and by some coincidence found itself for no explained reason near a corpse."

"That's not what I meant. I…"

"Or better yet," Torre interrupted. "It was brought to the island from somewhere else and dropped here." Belmont did not reply.

"Mr. Gaines," I said, turning to the chief ranger.

"How many times in the course of a day, week, month or even a year do you think screws such as these need to be replaced?"

"Probably not very often. I wouldn't even try to guess. I can find out if you really want to know," Gaines replied.

"A dozen times a year? Maybe once a month?" I asked again.

"That's probably too much. Again. The only ones with access to the crawlspace are our maintenance staff. They're generally thorough and make certain that every screw, nut and bolt is securely in place," Gaines added.

"This guy you mentioned before. The person in charge of the light brigade inside the torch. How seriously does he take his job?" I asked.

"He's relentless. He lives for the Statue of Liberty. We're fortunate to have men like him here. If he ever lost his job cleaning the torch he'd probably take the pipe," Will Johnson answered, his face breaking into a slight smile. "He's one of the most dedicated people I know."

"When would he have cleaned the torch before the body was found?" I asked.

"I'd have to check the records or ask him. I'd say within no more than a day or two before," the deputy chief ranger responded.

"When he last cleaned the torch. Can we assume that he would've have taken pains to make sure that every screw including the one that Sergeant Torre is holding was securely tightened? You just said he takes great pride in his work. Is that correct?" I asked. Gaines and Johnson nodded in the affirmative.

"That is a reasonable assumption, gentlemen, correct?" I persisted.

"How then, Goddamnit, can you account for the fact that this friggin' screw here wasn't properly tightened? Did it just drop out of the socket and onto the rug?" Torre shouted, as he purposely dropped the screw onto the floor. His face reddened.

"I don't know…I can't say." Gaines stammered softly as he again pulled his handkerchief from his back pocket.

"Is it a safe assumption Mr. Gaines, that the last person to close the hatchway door coulda been in a hurry to put all the screws into the holes. To put it another way, Mr. Gaines. Would ya say the last person to close the friggin' door was in no Goddamned condition to do so?"

"What're you implying?" Gaines shouted. Torre had goaded Gaines into losing control. Everyone waited for him to explode.

"You know what we mean. What I'm referring to, Mr. Chief Ranger, is the possibility that the dead woman was hiding inside the crawlspace for whatever reason. She felt sick from the heat and climbed outta the space when no one was around. Not having time to tighten all the screws, she accidentally left one outta its socket. She then made it to the second landing where she fell dead or unconscious. The screw dropped from her hand or outta her blouse onto the carpet," Torre shouted at Gaines. He held the screw up for everyone to see. The sergeant walked over to the chief ranger and extended his arms close to Gaines' face, the screw held tightly between his thumb and forefinger.

"Hold it Vin," I said.

"Here's another theory. Could the dead woman have been hidden in the crawlspace waiting for someone to let her out? When that individual did so, perhaps he or she panicked and neglected to tighten the fourth screw or didn't bother to replace it in the socket. In any event, it seems to me that there is complicity. I'm sorry to say this but a member of your staff was involved in or contributed to that woman's untimely death, Sam," The superintendent turned white He, too, removed a handkerchief from his pocket and he, too, wiped his face.

"Sergeant. You and Lieutenant Finnegan. You both have fantastic and vivid imaginations. What you outlined is possible but implausible. I'd go so far as to say your imaginations are playing tricks with you. You are so hard-up to solve this case that you're jumping to wild-assed conclusions that have no validity or merit whatsoever," Gaines said, trying to recapture the initiative.

"Let me continue, gentlemen. Point one. She could not have hidden in the crawlspace without anyone knowing it. Point two. She could not have been hidden there by anyone else without another member of the staff spotting it on the TV monitors. Third. We have regular patrols every evening. What you're saying is that all six of our rangers were involved in this unfortunate situation. Or they covered up for one of their colleagues. Why don't you lump Will Johnson and me into the equation? Make it an even octet." Gaines shouted.

"Calm down, Ron," Sam Belmont said to his chief ranger.

"We're discussing theories and possibilities here. These officers are not accusing anyone or implying any complicity. They are simply exploring the many possibilities," the superintendent added.

"I agree that she wouldn't have hidden in the crawlspace without a valid reason. If she did hide in the hatchway, someone who is familiar with the crawlspace and knew how to get in and out of it may have hid her. Furthermore, I agree that the person she conspired with must have been here that evening. But who is she or he?" Belmont thought out loud.

"Unless you, Ron, or William Johnson did it, and you both have valid alibis. This is preposterous," Belmont continued.

"What you are theorizing is that the screw did not just become loose…"

"A very distinct possibility," I responded.

"And you theorize that someone, perhaps a member of our ranger staff, was responsible for the woman's death directly or indirectly,"

"That's what we're thinking," Torre said.

Belmont stared at me for a moment.

"This is highly unusual," the superintendent said. He removed a pipe from his pocket and filled it with tobacco from a plastic pouch. He then removed a book of matches and lit the pipe.

"I know smoking inside the monument is against policy. But these are unusual circumstances," he said sheepishly.

"This is totally preposterous, gentlemen. These are serious charges to aim at one or more of my people. I honestly don't know what to believe or how to respond."

"How much space is there in the crawlspace? I'm six foot-two. Can I fit in there?" I asked.

"With difficulty, lieutenant. I couldn't fit in there and I'm not much shorter than you are," Gaines answered.

"Could the woman have fit into the crawlspace?" I asked.

Gaines rubbed his chin as he pondered the question.

"I don't know how tall or heavy she was. I didn't see the body. But if she was of average build and height, I think so."

"Can you be certain?" I asked.

"Yeah, I'd say so."

"How big is this guy who is head maintenance man for the torch?" I asked.

"About five feet-four inches. Maybe 130 pounds soaking wet," Gaines responded.

"Maybe about the same height as the woman and a few pounds heavier, you'd say. So if this maintenance man could fit into the crawlspace no doubt the woman could have. Is that correct?" I asked.

"Yes, I'd have to say so. That is an accurate statement," the chief ranger added.

"Any more questions?" Torre asked.

"Yes, Let me reiterate my question." It was Superintendent Belmont.

"Are you implying that the dead woman had access to the crawlspace leading to the arm and the torch? That someone, therefore, would have had to know she was here after hours?"

"That's our theory. Unless we prove otherwise, that's the way we're pursuing it, Sam," Torre answered.

"Again, that is totally preposterous. I resent any implication of impropriety by the men and women who work for me. I suspect and trust that you will not act hastily and make any arrests or statements to the press until and unless you have substantiated evidence. That will be all gentlemen," Belmont said curtly.

"I ain't implyin' nothin.' I'm not coming up with any wild-assed theories either. We ain't got no answers, no leads, no suspects, and no substantiated evidence. Our assumptions are based on professional experience and common sense. Right now, we're operatin' strictly on theory. As I told you before, we got a woman lying' in a Manhattan morgue who was found dead on the floor of the Statue of Liberty in the early morning hours. No bruise marks, no bullet marks or scars that woulda indicated a violent death. Our job. Lieutenant Finnegan's and mine, is to find out how she died, why she was here, and who in Hell she was. Until we get the answers we're lookin' for, Lieutenant Finnegan and I are gonna pursue every angle, every lead, and every fuckin' theory regardless of implications, inferences, or hard feelings. I ain't no social worker or psychoanalyst. I ain't here to win any personality contest. Lieutenant Finnegan and I have to solve a crime. So if you're pissed off, that's too Goddamned bad. Lieutenant Finnegan and Sergeant Vin Torre are gonna chase down every damn theory. Is that clear, Mr. Superintendent?" Torre shouted.

"Sorry for my outburst. I thoroughly understand," Belmont responded. He continued to draw on his pipe.

The superintendent turned to his chief ranger.

"Ron. What is your read on the police theories? Is what they said possible or plausible?"

Gaines looked around the room, as if weighing his words carefully.

Detective Torre's theory is totally unlikely." He stared at me as he spoke.

"Why would any of our staff let someone into the torch after hours? And why would the woman have been here? What could have been her motive or the motive of the person who let her in?"

Belmont turned to Will Johnson.

"What is your sense, William?"

"I wholeheartedly support Ron on this one, Sam."

Belmont turned to me. Did the medical examiner or any of your officers find anything in the woman's possession? Maybe an implement to unscrew the hatchway?" he asked.

"Nothing, Sam," I said.

"Let me add somethin' else," Torre interrupted.

"Let's assume the women hid in the crawlspace. How did she leave the area if the screws are on the outside of the hatchway cover? How could she loosen the screws? The only one who could have helped her was a National Park Service ranger on duty the night she died. Unless you come up with other ideas, that's the approach we are forced to pursue."

"She *had* to have help leaving the crawlspace," injected one of the Park Police officers who accompanied. me from Brooklyn. "Gaines is taller than she was and he needed a ladder to remove the screws. How could a five-foot woman tighten the screws if Gaines couldn't reach them from the floor? Someone with a ladder like that one or a step stool helped her."

I looked at the superintendent and then at Gaines again.

"Let me repeat, gentlemen. The woman hid inside the crawlspace. The ranger or whomever locked her in, let her out in a state of panic. Rushing to secure the space and hide all evidence, that person neglected to tighten all four screws or forgot the one that dropped near where the body was found," I said.

"Do you have any firm idea who could have done this horrible act?" Belmont asked.

"No. But we'll find out." Torre turned his back to the superintendent and Gaines. He walked toward the steps.

"I'm hungry. Let's get outta here."

Gaines removed the two-way radio from his belt and called the captain of the Park Service launch to alert him we were on our way.

"Hold the boat for me. I'll be a few minutes behind. I have to stop at my office. I'll meet you at the dock." Without waiting for a response, he ran down the steps, presumably to his office.

* * *

When Gaines entered the administration building, he ran past the dispatcher to his office. He locked the door, put his two-way radio into a small locker that he secured with a combination lock, and quickly dialed a number. When his wife answered, he explained that the investigation was getting hotter and that he was needed for the rest of the evening. He'd stay in his office to get some work done.

"I think I'll stay overnight with one of the rangers in Manhattan. Nobody you know. I'm not up to the long drive back to New Jersey. Besides, I don't know what time our meeting with the detectives will be over. They've been very helpful. Yes, we're collaborating with all the law enforcement agencies. Don't worry. I'll call you tomorrow. I've got a lot of work to do tonight. Tell the kids daddy loves them and make sure they go to bed at their normal time. I'll see you tomorrow." He blew a kiss through the receiver. The response he got from his wife was in the form of a question.

"Don't worry. I'm OK, hon. Speak to you in the morning." He then replaced the receiver onto its cradle. He quickly dialed another number.

"Hi. It's me, Ron. Will you be home tonight? I'm leaving the island with the gendarmes and I'll see you in about an hour. Can I come by? Great. No. A sandwich will be fine. The usual."

Gaines again replaced the receiver onto its cradle and stared blankly at the photograph of his wife and two children on his desk. He was sweating profusely. He was frightened and he fought desperately to suppress his fear.

He changed into jeans and a sweatshirt, closed the door to his office and rattled it to make sure it was locked. As he walked past the dispatcher, Gaines told him he would be on Liberty IV with the police.

"I'll be out of circulation until tomorrow morning. If there's an emergency, call Will Johnson."

He then walked toward the dock to where the police were waiting.

Chapter 15

Only the chug of the engine broke the silence aboard the park service vessel. Gaines sat quietly by himself at the back of the passenger cabin oblivious to our presence. When we docked in Manhattan, Torre called me aside. He wanted to talk to me. He lit a cigarette and leaned against his unmarked black Ford Victoria.

"I don't want anybody around. Let 'em all get outta here. I gotta talk to you," he said as he stared at the Statue of Liberty in the distance. He got into the car and flipped the switch on his door to unlock the passenger side. I was dragging. It was a long day and I had an hour's drive before I got home. But I wanted to know what was on Torre's mind so I got in. The car reeked of stale cigarette smoke.

"Don't you ever clean the ashtray in this car? How does the department let you get away with this shit? All Park Police cars are smoke-free.

Torre looked at me and laughed.

"You're tired, Mike. I won't keep you long. Just a few minutes. I promise. He opened the car window and flipped his cigarette onto the paved parking lot.

"Whatcha make of the meeting?"

"Is that what you wanted to ask me? I thought you had something important."

"Just want your opinion."

"That Gaines has balls."

"Whatcha mean?"

"I don't trust him one bit. But we don't have anything on him except arrogance. You can't arrest him for that. How long did you sit on your theory about the screw?"

"I don't know. It hit me one night. I was trying to sleep. The wife had already dozed off and I was having a hard time. I tried not to think. It hit me hard. The screw presented a question mark."

"I'd love to put a tail on Gaines. Where do you think he's going? You would have thought he'd have the boat captain drop him off in New Jersey so he could drive home. It's a long ride by subway from here," I said. I smiled to my colleague.

"Ten to one he's going to a lady friend's apartment, Mike," Torre said. I had thought about that but not seriously. Torre caught me off guard.

"Care to guess what I'm thinking?"

I sat silently for a moment and than uttered the initials JM.

"Like Jennifer Marcus?"

"I'd say so," I responded.

"Didja see the sweat pourin' off Gaines' face when I questioned him? I kinda got a kick out of seein' him squirm, that little jerk," Torre said.

"You'd make a hell of a prosecuting attorney." I gave him a gentle punch on his right shoulder.

"Yeah. Missed my calling, but it's too late for that now. Bein' a cop ain't that bad. I kinda enjoy what I'm doing and now I'm lookin' forward to windin' down and retiring. The kids are after me to take the missus on a long vacation and see the country. Vin Junior and Barbara are grown so it's just the two of us. I'm lookin' forward to spending more time with the missus. Ya know the crazy hours we keep. Like on this case. She's been a real trooper and I owe it to her. She's always been my best friend. Even when I was brought up on charges. She was always right there next to me. Never doubted my word for a minute. A better woman you'll never find. Good friend just had heart surgery and my wife insisted I go for a checkup. The doc said that I should smell the roses. and not push them up. I think it ain't such a bad idea."

"Any idea when you'll pack it in?"

"I ain't going nowhere until this Goddamned case is closed."

Torre changed the subject and asked if I thought Gaines was involved directly or indirectly in the woman's death.

"Probably not directly," I answered. "I think he knew something was happening. Maybe it's a case of don't tell me what you're doing. As long as you stay out of trouble and keep me out of trouble I don't want to know. That's my hunch," I said.

We sat for a moment and neither of us said anything.

"Whatcha think Gaines is gonna tell his friend when he sees her tonight?" Torre asked.

He lit another cigarette, put his Zippo back into his pocket, and rolled down the window to exhale the smoke.

"Probably not much. He'll tell her that you came up with the screw to the latch cover and matched it to the one that was missing. He won't go into any detail about the questioning and his thoughts about being a suspect. He's got too big an ego to let on that he's sweatin' right now," I said.

"Do you think Marcus is involved or implicated?" Torre continued.

"I don't know. I think they're both covering for each other and maybe someone else. But it's hard to say. We don't have anything concrete to go on. Just circumstantial evidence and our own thoughts."

Torre turned to me and laughed. It was now his turn to poke me in the shoulder.

"What didja think of the superintendent's denial that anything could happen on his watch? He's either naive to the facts of life or he's covering his ass so he can retire a proud man with a clean record."

I told the police sergeant that Sam Belmont had been around the

Park Service for many years and is politically savvy. He wouldn't have moved up the ranks otherwise.

"Bullshit Mike. Yeah. He's got a clean record and he's a decent guy. You know these types of choice assignments are political. It's who you know and not always what you know or how you do your job. Sometimes the guys who move up make safe decisions in their careers on accounta they don't want anything negative on their records. Ya know what I mean. No controversial decisions. Stay clean. Brown nose the regional director. Get your name in the paper for good things. Lay low and come up with a good rationale or denial when there's trouble. And above all. Always agree with what the guy on top says. It works in the NYPD and it sure as Hell works with the Park Service. In any bureaucracy, for that matter. Take my word for it. Look at me. I shoulda been lieutenant years ago. They'll never pin gold bars on a hard-assed cop like me. I do what I think I gotta do. Just shut up, do your job, and solve the case. If you bend the rules, don't tell me about it. Sure. They respect me. On the other hand, there's guys who hate my guts. They're jealous. But who says life ain't a bitch?"

"I wouldn't doubt for a moment that he knows where you're coming from. I think we got a good act from Gaines and Johnson," I responded.

"Let's go back to the beginning," Vin said.

"We know the woman must have come to the island on the last ferry and mingled with the crowd. Either she opened the hatchway cover door herself or got help. She hid, waiting for a designated time when someone could let her out."

I nodded in agreement.

"Good. Maybe she felt sick or was having difficulty breathing. Christ. It had to be at least one hundred degrees up there. Assume who ever closed the hatchway cover from the outside left the screws out or left them loose. When she jiggled the cover to get out, one fell to the carpet where it was found. She knows there's a ladder and where it's hidden. Or the person who helped her hide gets the ladder and puts the screws in place. Finding one missing he—"

"Or she," I interrupted.

"Okay. Have it your way," Torre responded sarcastically.

"Whoever rescrews the cover in place leaves one screw hole open since he or she can't find the screw. The next day the maintenance guy sees a missing screw and replaces it with one from supply. Even though it doesn't match," Torre continued.

"That leaves us with the following missing links," I added.

"Who hid her in the hatchway? What was she doing there? And what was her motive or the motive of whomever helped her into the crawlspace?"

"Correct, Michael."

Suddenly I had an idea.

"Try this on for size, my friend. You and I agree that Gaines is implicated to some degree. Maybe we're wrong. But let's run with the theory for a few minutes. I don't think he was actually involved insofar as the woman's death is concerned. But he must have known something was happening. He at least had an idea."

"Correct so far," the NYPD sergeant said.

"Now here's my thought. The woman was on the island to meet one of the rangers. She was invited specifically for a rendezvous," I added.

"What makes you so sure? Suppose you had the hots for one of the rangers and wanted to bed him down? Why wouldn't you do it in the guy's apartment or in a hotel room or somewhere else? Why would you screw around in the Statue of Liberty where anyone could see you? Christ, I seen it on park benches at Central Park and read in the papers about a couple arrested for screwing on a table at a McDonald's. But at a national monument?" Torre asked.

"That's just it, Vinnie. If you're young and looking for something different. Or doing what you shouldn't be doing where you shouldn't be doing it. Why in Hell do people bungee jump? Or sky dive? Or jump off the cliffs in Hawaii? For the Hell of it and for the thrill of doing something they know they can get killed doing," I persisted.

"How about sex in the world's greatest monument for the quick high?"

"So if we determine the sexual orientation of the woman who died we'll be able to zero in on who brought her to the island. Who invited her there?" Torre asked.

"Exactly. And, who contributed to her death or killed her?"

"The sexual orientation of the victim will let us narrow down the list of suspects from eight to two."

"You got it, my friend."

"Suppose, Michael, she was bisexual and coulda gone either way. Then we're at square one."

"That gets back to our question of where Gaines was headed when he left here."

"The Marcus woman may have been implicated in the woman's coming to the island. If she and Gaines are bedding down, she's gotta know something. Like a menage de trois."

If Gaines and Marcus are chummy, they discuss more than business when they're together. There are too many damned pieces to this puzzle and we ain't got all the pieces yet," Torre said. He flipped what remained of his cigarette out the car window.

We agreed nothing was certain.

Any one of the several male rangers could have had a reason to bring her there. Each has a good alibi but couldn't be ruled out. Similarly, the two women rangers also could be considered prime suspects; the woman who found the body and the ranger who hated subservient women. The more we tried to eliminate suspects the more each became an obvious suspect.

Finally Torre posed the sixty-four dollar question.

"Now where d'ya honestly think the Marcus woman fits into all this? Assume there's more than a working relationship between Ms Marcus and Gaines. We know she's from down south, alone in the big city. Maybe she needs the father figure. Someone to give her a shoulder to cry on. To confide in and chat with. Or sleep with in periods of loneliness. She gives the impression of being independent. She'll let nothing stand in her way in terms of career advancement. Sleeping with the boss couldn't hurt. On the other hand, he's a married man. She's sure, at least initially, of no permanent commitment. She's afraid of one. Didn't her parents split when she was younger?"

Torre tried to counter my argument but I stopped him short.

"And during one of their trysts she confides to Gaines that she's got bisexual or lesbian tendencies. She says she's seeing a lovely girl from out-of-town who shares her feelings and tendencies. The two women are tired of the same routine. They're looking for the ultimate climax which can't be achieved in a dingy Greenwich Village apartment. And he jokes about doing it in the Statue of Liberty. She takes him seriously so he tells her not to get caught. Maybe he even outlines how to do it."

"But..."

"They didn't know who would be patrolling the Statue that night. They didn't know the dispatcher wouldn't be checking the TV monitors at regular intervals. How in Hell could they hide her without anyone knowing it? Remember both Marcus and Johnson said that he opens the monument every morning. They had no way of knowing that he'd sleep in late that day and would assign Marcus to discover the body. Unless Marcus and Johnson were in on it together."

"Unlikely," I shouted.

"Will Johnson couldn't be. He's not that kind of guy. He wouldn't risk his career on some bimbo. He's single. As far as we know he has no steady lady friend. If he wants to screw around he can do whatever he wants in the city."

Torre scratched his head and lit another cigarette. He scratched his brow. He stared through the windshield.

"They knew the time of the patrols and that Johnson opened the monument at 7. So she could've stayed in the monument or on the island until about six before the next patrol. Gaines told us the torch ain't cleaned every day so Marcus or Gaines coulda realized that the morning the woman was hidden was not in the regular cleaning cycle. Whoever it was could've let the woman out of the hatchway just before the first Johnson patrol, to walk around and hide until the first boat arrived from Manhattan. Then mingle with the crowd and go back to the city or to Jersey City. Sound simple?"

"Let's not overlook the obvious," I said.

"Yeah," Torre responded. "I wonder what in Hell Gaines and Marcus are doing right now. This chief ranger with the swagger, spit and polish, and the heavy starch on his Goddamned uniform leavin' his wife and kids in New Jersey to screw around with some chick he works with. Imagine!"

"We don't have any proof that he's with her. Just speculation," I added.

"Yeah, just like my speculation about that damn screw from the hatchway door. Care for some coffee, Mike?"

I declined and walked to my car. I had the feeling that we were closing in on the solution but would have to wait for one of the rangers who was with the dead woman to make a mistake.

As I drove back to Brooklyn I thought of Ron Gaines and recalled how antsy he had become. I felt sorry for the superintendent because of the pressure from Washington and Congress. But for all I knew, my sympathy was misplaced.

Chapter 16

Gaines knew that he was making a mistake. He couldn 't control himself. He had to see her one more time in her apartment where they could be alone. The chief ranger was nervous and scared. What if his wife found out? Suppose someone saw him and asked him what he was doing in the neighborhood? What would he say? How would he react? Despite these fears, he was anxious and excited. He couldn't wait to hold her in his arms and feel her body close to his. "Get a hold of yourself," he repeated as he walked quickly toward the subway.

Gaines entered the South Street station and purchased two tokens. He imagined the token clerk was staring at him and laughing. He slipped one token into the pocket of his jeans, depositing the other into the turnstile. Thinking the police had put a tail on him, he casually looked behind him to make certain he was safe. Still he wasn't certain. Kneeling down to retie his sneaker, he thought he saw someone staring at him. His fears proved to be unfounded. Gaines walked down a flight of dingy stairs into the cavernous tunnel to wait for the Number 9 subway uptown. After an eternity, the uptown train arrived. He was the only person in the car. Normally he would have preferred other passengers around. But solitude freed him to focus and remember the entire dialogue that took place at the Statue of Liberty an hour earlier. He would fill in Jennifer Marcus with as many details as diplomatically appropriate. He was afraid that the police were onto something. Telling her would add pressure to her already fragile emotional state. Yet he felt obligated to keep her informed. She had a lot to lose if they ever found out. But he was in no mood for heated discussion if she panicked. He couldn't deal with her crying. Now that she was desperate, he couldn't afford to rock the boat any more than necessary. She was bound to pump him for information and re-assurance. That was fine but he couldn't or wouldn't lie to her.

By the time the train stopped at Christopher Street, some seven stations from South Ferry, passengers occupied most of the orange plastic seats. Gaines spotted a man, maybe in his thirties, leaning against a chrome pole in the middle of the subway car facing him. He read a folded newspaper. Gaines was scared that the stranger was a cop.

He left the car and climbed a long flight of steps onto Christopher Street. He glanced over his shoulder but saw no one. He then aimed east on Bleecker Street, to the brownstone walkup apartment where Jennifer Marcus lived. He again looked around him as he climbed the stairs, tripping on a crack in the cement. He grabbed onto an old wooden rail to prevent himself from falling. A young boy bouncing a basketball on the sidewalk below, ran up the stairs to help him.

"Ya OK mister?" he asked.

"Yeah. Fine, thanks."

"Can I help ya with somethin'? You look like ya's lost."

"No. Honest. I'm fine. Now why don't you go play basketball," Gaines said.

The youngster stared at him. He left without saying anything but continued to bounce the ball on the pavement.

Gaines stood motionless, staring at the boy until he was out of site. The ranger glanced up and down the street to ascertain no one else had seen him. He then took the steps two at a time until he was inside the front door. He leaned against the inside of the door, wiping the perspiration from his forehead. The sweat felt cold under his arms and his chest pounded. A mosquito hovered over him and he tried to flick it away with his hand. Gaines hesitated for as long as he dared before pressing the buzzer for Jennifer Marcus' apartment.

Before he could catch his breath, the buzzer responded with ferocity, to release the inner door. Gaines pushed it open, running up the three flights of stairs to his lover. The door was ajar so he entered unannounced. He looked around the small apartment but didn't see her. He began to panic.

"Jen. I'm here. Where are you?" he called.

"Be right out. I'm in the bathroom. Give me a couple of minutes. OK!" she shouted. Gaines was relieved.

"Jen. You shouldn't leave the door unlocked. You don't give a damn about your safety. You've got to be more careful. Lock your doors when you're alone."

"Ron, I was worried about you. You sounded...so nervous...so serious when you called. Are you all right?" Jennifer Marcus hooked her arms around his neck and hugged him tightly.

"Jennifer appeared as if from nowhere.

"Ron...You're sweating. Are you OK? Can I ask you how the meeting went or do you want to eat first? Is everything OK?"

The young woman wore a pair of loose fitting jeans and an oversized jersey with the words *University of Alabama.* She was shoeless but had on a pair of white athletic socks. Even without makeup she was attractive, Ron Gaines thought. And she was wearing his favorite perfume. The feint aroma sent chills up his spine.

"Everything's OK," he said, freeing himself from her grasp long enough to move to an old overstuffed armchair in the corner of the room.

Marcus jumped onto the old sofa opposite him and curled her legs under her body, her head on her arm, which rested on the arm of the sofa. She bit her fingernails and played with her toes, crossing and uncrossing her legs. Gaines hadn't seen her this tense in a long time.

"Come on Ron. What happened? Can't you see I'm a nervous wreck? Damn you. Tell me what happened." She began to cry.

"Cool it. Everything's all right." Gaines explained in general terms how the meeting went, how the police had produced the screw to the hatchway door, and tried to implicate one or more of the rangers.

"Did my name come up at all, Ron?"

"Why would it, Jen? No."

Gaines recounted Belmont's verbal explosion.

"The funniest thing was when Sam acted like it was so incredulous that something like this could happen on Liberty Island. He should win an Oscar for his acting," Gaines said. He broke into laughter.

"What's going to happen, Ron?"

"What do you mean?"

"Think they'll ever connect me to...you know, with Shirley..."

"Naw. How can they? The only ones who know are you and me and Shirley and our friend. Shirley can't talk. We must make sure he keeps his mouth shut. It was an unfortunate death and I'm sorry it ended that way. But life must go on."

Jennifer remained silently glued to the sofa. She continued to bite her nails and fidget with her toes. She suddenly got up and walked to the overstuffed armchair. She kissed Ron Gaines on the forehead. Going into the small kitchenette, she removed a sandwich from the refrigerator and put it on the small Formica covered table she had purchased from a used furniture dealer on her arrival in New York.

"I got your favorite beer. Come on. Have something to eat. You must be famished."

Gaines approached the table and sat down to eat his dinner.

Jennifer Marcus stood watching him enjoy the sandwich. She envied his wife and the fact that he had a permanent home to go back to. Yet, she was thrilled to be able to share him on those rare occasions when he could come up with a valid excuse to stay in the city. She was thankful for these moments but wondered how much his wife suspected. *What would she do if she ever found out?* Jennifer also thought about her and his future... *Their future*... Her body tingled. She fought the urge to hug him desperately. She didn't wish to disturb him while he ate.

Unable to control her emotions any longer, Jennifer gently massaged Ron Gaines' strong shoulders, caressing his neck and messing his blond hair. The chief ranger was oblivious to her attention. But when she glanced quickly at his jeans, she noticed that her caresses were registering. He resettled on the sofa, beckoning Jennifer Marcus to join him.

"I'll be back in a moment." Jennifer waved him off and walked into her small bedroom at the opposite end of the apartment. Five minutes later she re-emerged without her jersey. As she walked toward the sofa and Ron Gaines, she unsnapped her bra. Then she wriggled out of her jeans. She wore no panties.

Chapter 17

It was a rainy Monday morning and I was mad at myself because I didn't ask maintenance to check the windshield wipers on my sedan. Again, the little things were beginning to bother me. The blades were streaking the windshield and, consequently, it took me longer than anticipated to get to the office. My secretary handed me several messages.

"This top one is important. I'd respond to this call first if I were you," she said. Having been secretary and administrative assistant for more than fifteen years, she was able to prioritize messages in order of importance. She was correct most of the time.

"Sergeant Torre said it was important. Called at seven-thirty this morning before I had a chance to make the coffee."

I dialed Torre's number. An officer picked up the phone. He immediately transferred my call. Torre told me there was an identification of the corpse through dental records. He said the woman was from Boston but her last known address was New York City. I volunteered to send an officer to Boston to meet with the local PD up there and see what, if anything, they could find out.

"Who was she?" I asked.

"Name's Shirley Konowitz. Mean anything to you?"

"No. Should it?" I responded.

"Didn't think so. Nothin' in the phone book. We think she lived in the Village. Maybe shared an apartment with others. I'm sending a team to scour the Village. We got some pictures of her face at the Morgue. Our guys plan to show it around the neighborhood. Maybe we'll be lucky and come up with somethin' about her. I wanted to share this with you," he said.

I called Sam Belmont and told him about the new development. I urged him to keep it to himself. I then called the Park Service public relations officer, Mel Davis, and asked him to drop by my office at his convenience. Davis walked into my office without knocking about twenty minutes later and before I had a chance to invite him in he sat in front of my desk. I told him we got the identification and asked for his help. Davis smiled and just listened.

"I assume no one else knows about this except Torre and the medical examiner, you and now me?" he asked.

I asked Davis if he had a media contact who would publish a photo of the victim and ask for the public's help but would not divulge where the photo came from. Davis suggested a reporter in Newark.

"He'll get the story in the paper. I'll buy you lunch at your favorite restaurant if the other papers and the wire services don't pick it up. Once the story is out, I guarantee someone will read or hear about it who knew her and give you guys some clues," Davis said.

"How do we work the New York press? Won't they get angry if they see the story first in New Jersey?"

"Easy. My contact is the only reporter in metropolitan New York who has the Statue of Liberty as his beat. Sometimes that guy finds out stuff before I do. By the time I know what's going on he's already gone to press. He has an uncanny knack of getting the story before I can do a news release. That guy's a vulture when it comes to the monument. If someone asks, you don't know how he got the story. Let me handle it."

Davis said he would tell the New Jersey reporter to get details from the NYPD who got the initial ID. "He'll ask the sergeant if there's any photos. Hopefully, you guys will get some more info on the woman."

Davis was too intent on his purpose for small talk. He got up to leave. As he was about to walk into the hallway, he turned his head to me.

"Trust me. You know the story won't stay quiet too long. We might as well give it to a friendly reporter who can help us rather than someone who'll sensationalize it," he said. Davis left on that note. I called Torre and told him to expect a call.

The sergeant did get the call and cooperated with the reporter. The story broke and Davis was right. It was picked up by major wire services. Within 24 hours, my phone was ringing off the hook. Reporters and TV producers from throughout the world wanted interviews. They included the Associated Press, CNN, De Moines Register, Los Angeles Times, and of course, the New York press, network TV and the Boston Globe. They wanted updates, printable quotes and sixty-second sound bites.

I had alerted Sam Belmont to notify his staff to accommodate media with photograph requests of the monument. All other inquiries about the case were to be referred to me as the lead investigator. Torre also got phone calls. Since the Statue is federal property, he had all the calls referred to my office.

Meanwhile, the officer we sent to Boston was pouring through records in City Hall and police headquarters. We contacted all the colleges and universities within a fifty mile radius of Boston. At the same time, officers in New York visited businesses in lower Manhattan in an effort to find someone who knew the woman we hoped to identify.

Mel Davis returned to my office a day after the story broke in order to find out if we had heard anything as a result of the news stories. He hinted he was uncomfortable with the entire scenario.

"You know, Mike? I think it smacks of being an inside job. You've always leveled with me and I think I've never violated a confidence. But somehow I've got the feeling you're still holding back. I don't know why and can't prove a thing. But the fit just isn't right." I asked him to elaborate.

"I have a sneaking suspicion that the Konowitz woman wasn't just another tourist. She came to the island with someone. D'ya have any clues or ideas?"

I asked Davis how well he knew the staff. Especially Johnson and Gaines.

"D'ya think Johnson is involved or implicated?" Davis asked.

"Don't know. Torre does," I reiterated, displaying no emotion and waiting for his reply.

"Any idea why Johnson sent Jennifer Marcus into the Statue that morning?" I reminded Mel that our conversation was to be in the strictest of confidence.

"Never gave it any thought. Knowing Willie, I'd say it was pure coincidence. I'm a pretty good judge of character. I think Johnson is embarrassed by this whole scenario," Davis added.

I asked Davis what he knew about Jennifer Marcus. He repeated her name to himself several times in contemplation.

"Don't know. I never got to meet her on a one-to-one. I understand she's a good looker. Since she works nights I'm usually home with the wife so I can't say I really know her. When she's on days I'm usually not on the island except for meetings or special activities. So there's no chance for interaction. Are you implying some connection between her and the woman?"

"Don't read my mind," I admonished him.

I walked to the door and closed it. I told my secretary to hold all calls for awhile. I then sat down next to Davis.

"Let me level with you. Neither the NYPD nor I have any clues other than what I just told you. We've got a detective in Boston and local cops are scouring the Village and SoHo looking for anyone who may have known her. Between the photo in the papers and TV coverage thanks to you and your friend, we hope to gain something more definitive. Right now, we're still on a fishing expedition." I said.

Davis asked if there was anything else he could do. I told him to sit tight.

"If you're asked any questions, you know nothing," I thanked him for his help and he left.

Chapter 18

Johnson returned from his administrative leave. He was in his office before the shift change and was welcomed back by the entire night crew. It took him at least a half-hour to get to his office, having to greet, exchange hugs and handshakes and even a kiss from Jennifer Marcus. The deputy chief ranger was going over the morning ranger report by the time Ron Gaines came ashore onto the island.

"Welcome back, stranger," Gaines said as he barged into Johnson's office.

"Miss me?" Johnson asked.

"Are you kidding? Things haven't run as smoothly since before you were assigned here. You could have taken six months. Nobody missed you." Gaines smiled.

"Glad to know I'm appreciated. What's new with the investigation? I've been totally out of the loop. Bring me up to speed," the deputy said.

Gaines filled him in as the best he could. Frustratingly, not much had changed since his buddy took leave.

"What's new with you? How's the family. I miss the kids," Johnson continued.

Gaines pushed a chair close to Johnson's desk.

"Mind if I sit down?"

"Hell no. Go ahead. Why the secrecy?"

"What do you mean?"

"You pull your chair close to the desk, and you want to know what I mean?"

"Okay. I missed you, you son of a bitch. I really did."

"Wish I could say the same," Johnson responded.

"What do you mean by that?"

"Just giving you a taste of your own caster oil, that's all," Johnson said, breaking into a wide grin.

Gaines reciprocated.

"Something's bothering you, Ron. The murder? Something personal? Something you want to share with me?"

"I think I'm in trouble."

"What do you mean? The murder?"

"No, I'm clean."

"Lorelei? The kids?"

"No. I'm in the dog house and I beat up another woman."

Johnson stared at his boss.

"It's a long story. Lorelei's become cold. She's on the phone with her mom all the time. We sleep together but there's no…"

"Intimacy?"

"Yeah. That's it. We haven't made love in several months."

"The pressure?"

"Who knows. She's been acting strangely and asking a lot of questions. How come I'm away from the house so often and where do I stay when I tell her I'm in the city?"

"Does she have good reason to be suspicious? Does she know something?"

"I told her one night I was staying with you. She called your place and no one answered the phone. She got worried and called her father who told her it probably had to do with the investigation and maybe you and I were with the police."

"Does she know I was on leave?"

"I never told her. I figured what's the difference. I should have told her the truth," Gaines said.

"So what happened?"

"So I got home the next day and she started yelling and screaming. The kids started crying and ran to their rooms. They were scared."

"Damnit to Hell. You should have told me, Ron. I could have covered for you. Where were you?"

"I wasn't sure you were back. I would have called but it slipped my mind. I stormed out of the house. I missed the kids, but I purposely didn't call home. I was pissed at the wife. I was going to teach her a lesson. Anyway, I drove into Manhattan and went to one of those topless bars in Midtown. A woman picked me up and the next thing I knew I was in her apartment."

Johnson leaned back in his chair. He couldn't believe what he was hearing. He never dreamed that Ron and Lorelei were having problems.

"So she pours us some drinks and we're sitting around her place. An hour later we were in bed and she's laughing at me. I couldn't perform. I tried to explain I was tired, had a fight with my wife, and was under a lot of pressure. But she continued to mimic me."

"What did she say?"

"She laughed. 'For this I had to give up a coupla tricks tonight. Of all the guys in the joint I have to get somebody who can't do anything.' She continued to laugh and tried to kick me out of her place. Said she had to go back to work to make some money."

"Why'd you beat her up?"

"I slapped her. She hit me back and the next thing I knew she was on her back on the floor. I panicked and ran the hell out of the place. I don't even know the address. I should have called 911 but I wasn't thinking properly. Anyway, I drove around for awhile and came to my senses. I remembered the address so I stopped at a pay phone and called 911. Told them where to go. I then checked into a cheap hotel somewhere."

"Why do you think you're in trouble?"

"Damnit. Can't you see it? She's probably in some hospital somewhere telling the cops what happened and describing me. I've been reading the police reports in the papers every day but there's been nothing."

"Maybe she seemed more injured than she actually was. Maybe the ER bandaged her up and released her. The worse thing you can do is panic. You gotta relax, buddy."

"That's easier for you to say, you son of a bitch."

"Cool it, man. I just got back from administrative leave to clear my head. I don't need any of your crap. So cool it baby. Hear me?"

Gaines stared at his friend. He left the office.

Chapter 19

William Johnson was alone in his apartment writing a letter to his mother. He was interrupted by a knock on his door.

"Wait a minute. Be right with ya," he shouted from the kitchen table that he used as a desk. He looked at the Timex on his left wrist. It was almost nine forty-five in the evening. Standing outside was Skip Brandwyne.

"Mind if I come in? I have to talk to you for a minute?"

"Can I get you something?"

"No. I'm fine, thanks," Brandwyne answered.

"Everything okay? Any more bodies found this evening?" Johnson said in an attempt to break the ice and make the ranger feel comfortable. He sensed Brandwyne was tense and afraid.

"Mind if I sit down?" Brandwyne asked.

"Go right ahead. What brings you here?"

"This homicide is getting us all down. We're frightened. We're scared and we're all getting the feeling that we're under suspicion. You know what I mean. No one's telling us anything. We're getting rumor and hearsay."

"You know as much as I do if not more," Johnson said.

"I hear they've identified the body. At least that's what we read in the paper and it's all over TV. My folks called me the other day from California to find out what I knew about it," he said.

"Did the others ask you to come or are you here on your own?" Johnson sensed that Brandwyne was a committee of one and that the other rangers didn't know he had come to the apartment.

"There's speculation that she wasn't a casual visitor who got lost or who missed the ferry. That's why I'm here. I wanted to talk to you man-to-man. What can you tell me? Can you level with me, William?" Brandwyne asked beseechingly.

Johnson looked at him for a moment before answering.

"I've got no problem with your coming here. On the other hand, I've got a feeling you didn't come just to find out some information. If that's what you wanted you could have checked with the police. You want to tell me something. What's on your mind? Whatever it is, it won't leave this apartment unless you want it to. But I can't guarantee confidentiality forever. Eventually I may have to tell the authorities. It's your call."

Brandwyne sat staring at his boots.

Johnson broke the silence.

"Okay. I'm also up to my ass in rumors and suspicions. Now, damnit it. Why are you here? What's on your mind?"

"Mind if I take you up on your offer? Can I have a glass of water?" Brandwyne asked.

Johnson walked to the kitchen and took a bottle of water from the refrigerator. He poured a glass, which he brought back to the living room.

"Will, it's like this. I've got no proof and I'm not accusing anybody. But I think I know why the woman was here." Johnson was startled.

"How d'ya know?" he asked.

"I overheard some phone conversations a few weeks before. I thought nothing of it. But now I'm putting two and two together and coming up with six," Brandwyne said.

"Go on," Johnson said.

Brandwyne explained that he had arrived on the island early one afternoon and went to the concession area to get some coffee.

"While I was there, I overheard a conversation at one of the payphones." He then conveyed what he thought was a verbatim accounting of the conversation.

"Are you absolutely sure of what you heard and what you just told me?" he asked.

"The answer is yes. I'm no squealer, but I had to say something to someone. Hope you don't mind my coming here."

Johnson asked the ranger why it took him so long to come forward.

"'Cause I was scared. I gave this a lot of thought. Although I don't want to get anyone into trouble, I felt I couldn't keep it in any longer. You're the only guy around here I trust."

"What about the superintendent or Ron Gaines?" Johnson asked.

"I don't know. I feel more comfortable telling you. Hey wait a minute. You and Gaines are good friends. Are you gonna tell him what I just told you? Will I get into trouble?"

"I won't tell Gaines unless you want me to. What you told me will not be repeated to Gaines or any other ranger. But I have to report this conversation to the Park Police. I can't keep this information from them."

"Are you sure you won't implicate me?" Brandwyne repeated. His hands tightly clutched the glass of water.

"Absolutely. Not in any way. I can promise you that unless you tell what you told me to others. Lieutenant Finnegan probably will want to talk to you within the next few days. I'll recommend that he do so off the island," Johnson said.

Johnson asked Brandwyne if he was certain no one saw him listening to the phone conversation he had described. The ranger assured him that to the best of his knowledge he was undetected.

"If what you've told me results in an indictment or arrest, you may have to appear in court and testify. But you've got my word. I won't divulge my source of information to anyone," Johnson repeated.

Johnson put his arm on Brandwyne's shoulder and walked him to the apartment door. When Brandwyne left, Johnson walked to his sofa and sat down. He scratched his cheek, rubbed his eyes, and closed them momentarily in deep thought.

"What next?" he asked himself. Where in God's name is this going to lead? How'd I get involved?" Johnson returned to the kitchen table and the unfinished letter. He reread what he had written before the interruption and put the pad back onto the table. He then grabbed a piece of yellow lined paper from the notepad, walked slowly back to the sofa, and wrote some notes about his conversation with Brandwyne. He then folded the note into quarters, put it on his dresser next to his wallet and keys, and prepared for bed. He would not sleep well that night.

Chapter 20

Lorelei Gaines read bedtime stories to the two children and tucked them into bed. After kissing them good night, she returned to the spotless kitchen. She washed the dinner dishes, put everything away, and joined her husband who was reading the evening newspaper in the living room.

"Good dinner, hon. Your meat loaf's still terrific," he said.

"Thanks, darling," she responded. Mrs. Ron Gaines was relieved that her spat with her husband was resolved and forgotten. For the kids' sake it was better this way. At least, for the time being.

"How was your day?" he asked.

"Uneventful. I bought the kids new sneakers. I can't believe the prices. It's out of sight. When are you getting your next step increase? We're going broke keeping the kids clothed and fed," she said.

"I don't know. Remember when we were kids? One pair of sneaks lasted us the whole school year. Now it seems they don't even last a term," he responded.

"Tell me about it. You don't write the checks," she said, giving her husband a loving poke in the ribs.

"It's going too far. You can't tell me all the clothing companies don't meet once a year and determine how long their clothes will last or how well the sneaks will wear before having to be replaced." She sat on the arm of the chair. She teasingly tickled her husband and kissed the top of his head.

Gaines looked up at his wife. A big smile appeared on his face.

"What's bothering you, Ron? You're not yourself."

"Nothing. Why?"

"I don't know. You're not acting right. You don't have the patience with the children that you used to have and we...we...we don't talk anymore. And do what we used to do when we were alone. Things are different."

Gaines put his hand on his wife's knee and looked at her.

"I've been under a lot of stress lately. That homicide and the rangers all talking about it. And the police don't think I'm moving fast enough with the investigation. Damnit, Lor. It's only Will and me. The regional office wants to send a team down to New York. I'm fighting it. They wouldn't know what to do or anything about New York or the island. And the police and Park Police aren't cooperating that much. Let me tell you something. I don't think they've got the commitment. They think that Will and I are sufficiently staffed to do the investigation. All they're doing is criticizing. I keep telling them we're moving as fast as we can. Even the superintendent is getting on my case. He's getting all kinds of pressure from the regional office and Washington and he's in a state of panic. I keep telling them there's little I can do beyond what we're doing. But the investigation is moving forward."

"You poor dear. I feel so sorry for you," Lorelei Gaines told her husband as she rested her head on his chest.

"I didn't realize all the problems you are having. And all your responsibilities. I'm sorry I've not been the best wife. I've not shown you enough sympathy. You're a good sport always putting up with my being on the phone to my mother. But it's lonely around here when you're not around. And you've been away so much at night on the awful case. You must have some wonderful friends to allow you to stay over at their apartments when you work late. I'd like to meet them some time. Maybe when this case is solved we can have a big party and invite them all over here to show them our gratitude. Wouldn't that be nice?"

Ron sat there stunned. He never expected his wife's reaction. He wondered whether she was testing him or she knew something and wanted to get his reaction. He wouldn't be surprised if his mother-in-law put Lorelei up to this.

"Yeah. That would be very nice," he responded.

"You don't sound enthusiastic."

"It's just that I'm tired. Who knows when we'll crack this case. Several of the guys want off the island but we can't let them go until we find the murderer. By the time we do, maybe they'll have put in their applications for new jobs. I know some of them are already completing the paperwork so all they'll have to do is send them out."

"Maybe we can do it soon after this is over. You know, before they've had a chance to relocate. I feel guilty not being able to reciprocate for all of their kindnesses. Do you realize the fortune it would cost if you had to stay in hotels? They don't pay per diem since you're not on travel status."

"Yeah. I know. I am lucky, Gaines said. He thought desperately for a way to change the subject. He was becoming nervous.

"I called the Park Police and NYPD for help. You'd think they'd assign a team to help me. No. All they do is send Finnegan and that Torre clown. He shoulda retired ten years ago. He's over the hill. He reminds me of the self-made man who adores his creator." Gaines smiled.

"How's the staff reacting? Is Will holding up under the pressure? You don't talk about him anymore like you used to," Gaines' wife said.

"We're all under a lot of pressure. My staff thinks they're under suspicion. And you can tell by the expressions on the faces of the visitors that every time they see a ranger in uniform they think he or she did it. Until the police help me solve this damn case, I'm not going to be myself. Please bear with me. We're closing in on a suspect and we hope to resolve things soon. Do you realize how many visitors ask us if it is safe to be on the island? It's like there's a murderer running loose and lurking under the torch waiting for another victim. And the Park Police and New York police. If they know something, they're not telling us. Damnit, hon. I'm chief ranger responsible for law enforcement. I asked for their help. Now I sometimes know less than the people who work under me."

His wife remained silent. She continued to run her fingers through his hair.

"It's not you or the kids. Believe me. It's the pressure of the job and that damn murder." he added.

"Would it be better if *you* put in for a change of assignment? Maybe to another park miles away from here?"

Gaines looked at his wife.

"You don't want to leave your parents. They love to see the children and you've always been close with them. How do you think they'd react if we moved away? It wouldn't be fair to them or to you and the children."

"Did you ever hear of airplanes, Mr. Gaines? They could visit us. Why couldn't we fly home for holidays and when the kids are off from school? I'd hate to leave. If it meant less stress for you I'm willing to make the sacrifice." Lorelei Gaines began to cry.

"The superintendent insists that he wants me continue to run the investigation. He personally told me so. How can I put in for a change of assignment when I'm in the middle of the probe? I'm too important to the case. I'm the lead investigator. Do you know what that means? When the case is resolved I'll be in a good bargaining position to name my park. This is the biggest case of my entire law enforcement career. I'll never duplicate the experience. I sure hope I never again have to"

"I'm afraid, Ron. I sometimes get the feeling that our marriage is going to Hell. What can I do to keep us together as a family? I just want us to be happy. You know that," Lorelei Gaines sobbed.

"What makes you think our marriage isn't strong? I love you and the kids more than anything in the world and will never do anything to hurt you. You know that."

"I think I do. Ron. It's just that…I don't like seeing you the way you are. You're not the same Ron Gaines I married out of college. Maybe it's my womanly instinct. There's something more going on and I don't know what it is. That's what scares me."

"Have the kids said anything?" Gaines asked.

"Once in awhile they say something about how you're not the same jovial dad they once knew. I tell them you're under a lot of pressure and that things will be different. They're too young to tell them about that woman on Liberty Island. I don't go into specifics. They wouldn't understand. They're old enough to know there's something not right," she said.

"What about your parents?" Gaines asked.

"They try to stay out of our affairs and I don't say anything to them. But…"

"But what?" Gaines interrupted.

"My mother senses there's something wrong."

"What do you mean?"

"She commented the other day that I don't look right. She asked me if I'm getting enough sleep. Mom suggested I go to the doctor. Maybe take some vitamins. She told me about a multi-vitamin a friend of hers takes. Swears it works great. Never felt better. Mom said I'm not acting as happy as I used to be and that she felt that I'm worried about something. She even asked me if our marriage is still OK. I assured her that everything is fine."

"Damnit, Lorelei. Doesn't she read the papers or listen to the radio? My name's not in the news. However, like I told you, I'm working behind the scenes and the police and Sam Belmont are depending on me to solve this damn case. I'm on the phone several times a day with them, and with that police detective from Manhattan. Does she realize the stress her son-in-law is under? What does she think I do all day? Sit around with a counter and just count everyone who gets off the

Goddamned ferry?" he shouted.

"Mom knows all about it. In fact she even clipped the story from the Newark paper about the police trying to find out information about the poor woman. She even wondered why police were quoted since you're leading the investigation and you're responsible for law enforcement on the island. The reporter quoted a Sergeant Torre extensively but your name was omitted. She thought that was strange. In fact, she even asked me if I'm certain you're working on the case and my father asked me how you can investigate a case involving your own staff."

"Tell your mother that when the reporter called me to follow up on the tip, I sent him to Manhattan. I felt it wouldn't help our case to have park personnel quoted while the investigation is going on. Besides, you know the way I try to avoid publicity whenever I can. There's nothing to worry about. Tell her that once this case is solved she'll inherit two grandchildren for a few days so I can take you on a second honeymoon," Gaines said as he stared into his wife's eyes.

"I can't wait, sweetheart," Lorelei responded.

"Neither can I," he said.

"Promise?"

"Absolutely. Cross my heart," said Ron Gaines as he broke into a broad grin.

His wife got up from the arm of the chair. She grabbed her husband by his hands, pulled him up from the chair, and hugged him tightly.

"I love you husband," she whispered into his ear.

"I love you, too, wife," he whispered as he pulled her toward their bedroom.

"I know I haven't been good to you, Ron. Let me show you I still know how."

Chapter 21

"Pick up the phone, Mike."

"Your line secure?"

"Yeah, why?" I asked.

"Got some more interesting information," Torre said.

"This'll blow your mind, Michael. Since I was quoted in the papers my phone's been ringing like you won't believe. I've been sending most of the calls to you. But this one got through to me and I think it's important." Torre spelled out the information in excited bursts.

"Say that again. Are you sure?" I responded.

"I'm sending a detective to Rhode Island this afternoon to follow up the lead. I got the woman's name and phone number and she said she'd be glad to talk to us but can't come to New York."

"Now repeat what you just told me," I said.

Torre explained that he received a call from a woman in Providence who claimed she went to college with Shirley Konowitz and that she had an affair with her when she was a junior and the dead woman was a freshman.

"Ya sure you got the story straight and she isn't some crackpot?" I asked.

"This woman said there was a party at her apartment. It was late and Miss Konowitz didn't want to go home alone at that hour of the night so she stayed. After they did the dishes, they smoked some joints. Then they chatted and got ready for bed. Mike, this woman didn't leave out too many details. She even remembers what they were wearing at the party, and described the Konowitz woman perfectly. She told me where to look for birth marks," Torre said.

"How many encounters did these women have?" I asked.

"She said they saw each other a few times and then went their separate ways. This woman's now married and has a couple of kids."

"So it coulda been a short fling. She coulda gotten drunk or was high."

"It's a lead worth pursuin'. It sheds some light on the case and even if it goes nowhere we gotta follow it up," Torre said.

I tried to collect my thoughts.

"Are you still there?" I asked. When he answered in the affirmative I began to think out loud.

"Ms Marcus knows more than she's saying. Gaines is getting screwed. If he doesn't know what's going on, he ain't doin' his job. If he does, he's an accomplice. Ms Marcus invites the woman to the island. She doesn't expect her to die."

"She didn't expect that Johnson would ask her to inspect the monument either. Maybe Johnson *is* in on this."

"I doubt it."

"Ms Marcus asks her lover for help and he demands we drop our investigation. He's afraid we're gonna implicate him. I wish I was twenty years younger and had more guts. Remember that case about two years ago when I got a confession from that punk in Manhattan who beat his ex-wife to a pulp although she had an order of protection from the court? The case was dead until I got involved. Wham. We solved it in less than a week."

"Yeah, I remember. The department reprimanded you because the suspect claimed you pistol-whipped him. None of that bullshit here.

This is federal property and I'm not standing for any intimidation. We're going to play by the book."

"What makes you so Goddamned righteous? Sometimes you gotta deviate from the rulebook. Yeah, I may have been hard on that guy but he's serving time and rotting in jail. That's the bottom line, ain't it?"

"Look Vinnie. I'm not going over all the reasons but they all are suspects."

Torre and I explored several other theories and I reiterated my doubts about the source in Rhode Island. I couldn't believe that a married woman with children would initiate a phone call to a New York City police detective to unearth something in her own past that could prove to be embarrassing to her. I then changed the subject and asked what the detective uncovered in Boston. "Konowitz had no family. Her parents were deceased. She had few friends in Boston and no enemies, and appeared to be a typical innocuous and boring young woman who comes to New York for fame or fortune and finds neither. There are thousands of Shirley Konowitzs throughout New York with the same story. They come from all over the world and eventually get lost in the shuffle or step off the moving platform into oblivion," I said.

"Yeah, Mike. But when was the last time one of your innocuous young women seeking fame and fortune earned the distinction of dying in the bowels of the Statue of Liberty?" Torre asked.

I asked him for the name of his source in Rhode Island. He identified her as Sarah Ryan-Brown. He gave me her address and phone number.

"She said she's happily married and her husband knows nothing about her relationship with Ms Konowitz."

When I got off the phone, I called a retired cop I hadn't spoken to in several years who now ran his own private investigation agency in Pawtucket. After a few minutes of small talk I asked if he had read about the death at the Statue and told him a few details. I asked him to put out some discreet feelers to turn up what he could about Mrs. Sarah Ryan-Brown. I explained that I couldn't officially hire him but would make it up to him the best I could.

* * *

Torre called me back three days later to tell me he was on his way to my office. He handed me a manila envelope as soon as he entered my office.

"Our detectives are picking up a lot of information. You wouldn't believe how many people read the papers and watch the ten o'clock news. We got nothin' of any substance in Boston as you know but Bill Jessup, one of my detectives, comes to my office yesterday and says he got a lot of stuff here. He visited a number of joints in the Village. You know coffee shops and boutiques and places like that, and he shows the picture of Miss Konowitz around." I listened as Torre continued.

"A counterman at one of those coffee shops tells Jessup that the Konowitz woman frequented the place. She was a steady customer. This guy said she was a nice woman who minded her own business. Occasionally spoke to others who she recognized, and she was always kinda short of cash but always paid up her bills."

"Is that why you came here?" I asked.

"No wait, there's more. This'll knock your jockey shorts off. Listen closely."

Torre explained that this counterman told Jessup that about a year ago the woman he recognized as Ms Konowitz, was sitting in the restaurant minding her own business and reading a newspaper. She ordered some pastry and coffee and had apparently left her wallet in her apartment or had run short of cash like she usually did and the clerk was going to put it on her tab. Another young woman came into the restaurant, ordered a donut and coffee, and paid Miss Konowitz's bill as well as her own. She then whispered into the clerk's ear that she didn't want the other woman to know about it. When Ms Konowitz left the restaurant the other women followed her, or at least walked in the same direction.

"Do you think the counterman could identify the woman?"

"We're a step ahead of you, Mike. Bill already asked that question and was told no. All he knew was that she was attractive and about the same age as the victim."

"Could have been any one of thousands of young women," I said.

"Okay. I agree, but the incident remained in the guy's mind since he never saw anyone pick up the tab for a stranger and so secretive like," Torre said.

Sensing that he wasn't getting too far with me, Torre continued.

"So Jessup did some checking on his own and went from door to-door to every building superintendent within a ten-block radius. He found Ms Konowitz's apartment and spoke to the landlady. He asked if she knew anything or had seen anything. He didn't find out too much. Some occasional visitors to the apartment. Rent usually paid on time. She was late a few times but always came up with the money within a week. She kept to herself and never gave the landlady any problems."

"What about friends?" I asked.

"The landlady said she saw two people regularly. One was a young man who came by to pick up Ms Konowitz. They usually left together. She doesn't know whether he ever slept over, but the landlady said she never really cared. The usual. Ya know, claims to see and know nothin' but probably can tell you how many socks in the tenant's sock drawer at any time."

I knew the type well, "I said

"Then she told Jessup there was a woman who came to the apartment often and sometimes slept overnight," Torre said.

I asked if she gave the detective a description and Torre responded.

"Get this one, Mike. The landlady describes this woman's build, height, color of her hair…"

"Don't tell me, Vin. She resembled Jennifer Marcus," I interrupted.

"You got it man," Torre said as he slapped his fist on my desk.

"I bet there are hundreds of women resembling Jennifer Marcus in New York City," I responded.

"You're probably right. But get this one. There's more. A coupla times the landlady is sweeping the vestibule of the building and this woman comes by to visit Miss Konowitz and says hello. She speaks with a southern drawl."

Before I could respond, Torre reached into his pocket and pulled out a pack of cigarettes. Taking one from the full pack, he took his Zippo from his pants pocket and lit it. We watched the smoke swirl above him toward the ceiling. Neither of us said anything.

"We have only circumstantial evidence. Now we have to place Miss Marcus at the scene of the crime and tie her into the other woman. Then we may have a case. We don't know, in fact, whether Jennifer Marcus paid Miss Konowitz's coffee tab that night at the restaurant. I've got reason to suspect she did. Now we have to prove it," I said.

I suggested we confront Sam Belmont.

"Wait twenty-four hours." Torre asked me where I thought Ron Gaines fit into this sequence of events.

"We can't rule him out as a suspect. Remember when we left the island and we saw him walking to the subway?" he said.

Chapter 22

Gaines was reviewing notes from a meeting he had earlier in the day with William Johnson. They had discussed a number of issues involving security, administration, and Shirley Konowitz. Johnson avoided discussing Skip Brandwyne's visit to his apartment. A gentle knocking on the door interrupted Gaines.

"C'mon in. Door's open," he shouted.

"Mind if we chat?" It was Jennifer Marcus.

"I can come back later."

"Sit down." Gaines pointed to the chair opposite his desk that Johnson had vacated.

The chief ranger had made up his mind that his relationship with the young park ranger would from that point on be totally businesslike. Things had to change despite what had gone on between them in the past and their feelings towards each other. He had to cover his ass to protect his career, his marriage and his life. On the other hand, he didn't want to hurt Jennifer.

"What's up?" he asked casually.

"Haven't really seen you in awhile. Just thought I'd come in and catch up," the young woman said.

"How's the world treating you, Ron?" she asked.

"Fine."

"Anything new on the case?" she asked.

"What d'ya mean?"

"Have you learned any new developments from the police?"

"You know as much as I do, Jennifer," Gaines responded.

"My, you're acting strangely," she shouted.

"What makes you think that?" he asked.

"So cool. So straightlaced. So businesslike. So Ron Gainesish...You're living up to your spit and polish reputation."

"How do you expect me to act? Want me to grab you and kiss you as if we're lovers? I bet you're dying for me to do that. Then you'd bring me up on sexual harassment charges. This is my office and we're both on duty. In case you forget, I'm the damned chief ranger on this island twenty-four hours a day, three hundred and sixty-four days a year. Let me remind you that you are a ranger sworn to help me protect this place. And you want me to act anything but businesslike in my office? You must be kidding. Why are you here?" he barked.

"The same reason I was here a few weeks ago. The reason you came to my apartment after the police returned to the island and questioned you. Want me to go on?"

"I don't know what you're talking about. Look. We've got to cool it for awhile. I don't know any more than you do. I swear it. But for the good of both of us we've got to keep our distance," Gaines whispered.

"As far as the public, the police, and the staff are concerned, you're just one of dozens of rangers assigned to guard the Statue of Liberty. Maybe when this case is laid to rest things can be different. For the time being we've got to stay away from each other except on official business. You've got to go through the chain of command. Through Will Johnson and not directly to me."

"What about your wife?" Jennifer asked.

"What about her?"

"Is she on to something?"

"About what in particular?"

"You know. Us."

"No," Gaines lied. He suddenly remembered his wife's comments, and her telling him about her mother's concerns.

"Are you sure?"

What in the world are you talking about? Is this Twenty Questions?" Gaines stopped short.

Jennifer Marcus stared at her boss and lover. Grabbing a tissue from the box on the desk, she wiped her eyes. She quickly grabbed a letter opener from the desk and threw it at Gaines. It missed him, landing on the floor behind his chair.

"You fucking macho pig. Who are you shouting at? How many other women are you screwing besides me? I should call your wife and tell her about her husband. I should tell her what a saint he ain't. It would be the most enjoyable long-distance call I've made in a long fucking time."

Before Gaines could stop her, Jennifer Marcus grabbed a glass paperweight from the desk. As she rose from the chair, she flung the paperweight to the ground and stormed from the office, slamming the door behind her. The paperweight splattered into hundreds of tiny pieces.

The chief ranger continued to sit at his desk, head in his hands. He stared at the photograph of his wife and children. He grabbed a tissue and wiped his forehead. He was perspiring profusely. Where was he going and how would he get out of this mess? A tear trickled down his cheek.

Chapter 23

"Mr. Johnson is here to see you, lieutenant."

The deputy chief ranger called me about about his meeting with Brandwyne. He walked into my office and after admiring the photographs tracing my career in Washington, he clutched my hand in both of his. It was the handshake of a man who was comfortable with himself and confident of what he was going to tell me. I offered him coffee or a soft drink. He declined.

"Listen. I've been sitting on something for three or four days that I didn't know what to do with or how to handle. I can't keep it to myself any longer. You're the only guy I can think of to get things off my chest."

Johnson paced momentarily.

"Look. This may be hearsay or fact. I haven't made up my mind. Before I go ahead, I swore to the person who told me that I would tell no one and I don't want to violate that promise. Try to keep my source out of the picture if you can."

I promised to do what I could but could make no assurances until I knew what he was going to tell me.

"It was around nine or nine thirty at night. I'm in my apartment writing some letters and there's this knock on my door. When I open it, there was one of the young rangers who was on the island the night the woman died."

"Who was it?" I asked.

"Bear with me, Mike. I'll tell you when I finish what I came here to say."

"One of the rangers we interviewed right after the body was found?" I asked.

Johnson nodded affirmatively.

"Anyway, this ranger came to my apartment and said he had to talk to me, ya know like I'm talking to you now. But he was a lot more nervous than I am. So I tried to calm him down. We made small talk, I got him a glass of ice water and we just chatted. He proceeds to tell me he'd overheard another ranger on a pay phone talking to someone about coming out on the last ferry and mixing with the crowd and hiding somewhere after the last boat had left. He said that's all he heard since he didn't want to look conspicuous by hanging around the public phone area in his Park Service uniform."

"Did he identify the person?"

"Yes, he did. He also told me the person spends a lot of time in the chief ranger's office. There are rumors that something was going on besides official business."

"Ya mean Gaines?" I asked.

Johnson nodded again.

"I think you once told me that you're very close. Is that correct?" I asked.

"He's my best friend in the Park Service. He and his wife invite me to their home quite a bit. I love their kids. Sometimes I sleep over."

"Tell me about his family?"

"Lorelei's a class lady. In fact, I sometimes think she's too good for her husband. She comes from a good family, too. Her father is an MIT graduate. Retired a few years ago as an executive with AT&T. He's very astute. His wife taught school in South Jersey for many years. Lorelei is their only child. They dote on her and the grandchildren.

She's an adoring wife and wonderful mother. Their house is immaculate. But just between the two of us, Mike. I don't know what she sees in that schmuck."

"D'ya think they have a good marriage?" I asked.

"Ya mean do I think one of them is fooling around? I don't know. Ron adores his kids and his wife but the commuting from New Jersey is getting to him. And he's confided in me that the pressure of the job, especially since the murder, is taking its toll. Sometimes when we're working late he'll stay in the city. I never ask where he stays. It's none of my business. If he wants to tell me he can. If not, I say or ask nothing."

"What do his in-laws think about him?"

"I honestly can't say. I think that if his father-in-law found out that Ron was fooling around, he'd call in some political chips and have Ron shipped on the next plane to the northern part of Siberia. And I ain't kidding. He would do it. If he didn't kill Ron first."

"Has Gaines ever hinted to you that he's having marital problems?"

"Whoa. Now we're getting personal and I'm getting uncomfortable. I'll try to answer your question. No more. Okay? Once in awhile he tells me as a friend that he'd love to move to another park out west. He's from the Midwest. The problem is Lorelei is very attached to her parents who live near them. So my guess is that a transfer is out of the question. It would break the grandparents' hearts."

"You mean the bastard really has a soft spot in his heart for somebody?"

"That's it, man. Ron's between that rock and the proverbial hard place. He doesn't need a body being found and rumors about his fooling around or getting too chummy with…"

"Jennifer Marcus," I interrupted.

"Yes," Johnson whispered.

I asked him what he thought Gaines would do. Johnson admitted he had no clue.

"I'm single and unattached so I can move at any time, but I don't know what I would do if I had a wife and kids and a mortgage. Frankly, I don't know what I'd do either."

I repeated my earlier question about Gaines' marriage and Johnson said that without a doubt he thought it was strong and solid.

I asked him whether the ranger who was seen at the phone in the concession area was a woman.

"Either you're perceptive or you know something. The answer to your question is..." There was a pause.

"The answer to your question, Mike, is maybe."

"Could the ranger making the phone call have been Jennifer Marcus?" Johnson just nodded.

Silence.

"D'ya have any idea what happened the night the woman died? This is too important. Level with me," I said.

"I'm trying to put this together but I don't get it. I was there with you when the sergeant grilled Gaines about the missing screw and the woman hiding in the crawlspace. And I've heard all the same rumors saying the woman was hidden there by one of us."

"How soon before the death did you say the phone conversation was overheard?" I asked.

"The ranger didn't tell me. I'd guess not more than a few days. Maybe a week at most. Could even have been a day or two before. I really don't know."

I asked Johnson to tell me again what he knew about Miss Marcus.

"Very little. I told you everything I know about her and it was all favorable. I can't speak for her personal activities. None of my business. I try to get along with everybody on the staff and stay out of their personal lives. It's better that way. The National Park Service is a small agency. Everyone already knows too much about everyone else. If you want, I could get her personnel file again. You've already seen it. She's been a good ranger. Conscientious, hard working and all that crap."

I asked whether he thought she could have been involved in or contributed to Ms Konowitz's death.

"That's a heavy charge, Mike," Johnson responded.

"I'm not in any position to say. That's your job. You're investigating the case. Not me."

"Your honest opinion."

There was a long silence.

Johnson stood and walked around the room again. His hands were in the back pockets of his faded jeans and he studied the photos on my walls once more. He returned to where he had been sitting but continued to remain mute. I sat patiently trying to read Will Johnson's mind.

"Mike, ya want my honest opinion?"

"Yes."

"I don't know. Any of the rangers that night could have been involved. Jennifer could have played an active role. She could have just been the go-between for someone else. If you want me to say she might be involved, based on what my informant told me in my apartment I gotta say yes. We all could have been. Even me," Johnson said.

"Where does Gaines fit in to this?" I asked.

"Beats me. I'm sounding like a broken record. My heart says definitely nowhere but my gut says maybe. I guess it's possible he knew something. Ron's got a good marriage, a super wife and great kids. He's in an enviable position. He's got everything to live for. Why would he fool around with another woman? I'm totally confused. Gaines is an unpopular guy. I'm the first to admit it despite the fact that he's my buddy. He's hated by just about everyone but me and his family."

I grabbed a pencil from my desk and twirled it between my fingers. I listened to what Johnson was relating but I said nothing.

"I ain't tellin' tales outta school. I've told him more times than I can count not to be so hard-assed. Christ, I remember he had a young ranger crying 'cause he shouted that the kid's shoelace was untied. It was in front of visitors. I heard about it and asked Gaines why he humiliated the young man. That bastard just laughed and walked away."

I continued to twirl the pencil.

"Another time Ron threatened to fire a maintenance man whose pants were stained. The guy tried to tell him he was working in the boiler room and didn't have a chance to change but Ron didn't want to hear it. I was scared Bill was going to kill Gaines right there. Want me to go on? I can tell you plenty of other stories."

"He plays no favorites. He's screwing around on his wife. A real schmuck," I said.

Johnson got up and leaned his elbow on my desk.

"You should have seen the fights we had over Vietnam. I'm not a flag waver. I do my job and don't care what anyone else thinks. I volunteered to serve my country and shipped overseas right after advanced infantry training at Fort Benning. I got a Purple Heart. Not many people know it. I like it that way. That's why I don't take bullshit from anybody about the war. I lost too many of my buddies. Too many good men never came home. We didn't give a damn if you were white or black, from the south or the north, were a poor kid or had several college degrees. We needed each other. And we never came down hard on anybody unless they were a real fuck-up. Did you know that Gaines ran away to Canada to beat the draft? That flake never spent a day in uniform. When I first got here we'd fight like Hell over Vietnam. Finally I said one day I didn't want to hear about it any more. I was the first and last guy to stand up to him. We've gotten along fine since."

"Do you ever discuss his personal life?"

"I told him how a buddy at the furniture company in North Carolina saved my life when I was high on drugs. I used to tell him now it's my turn to help a friend. I said screwing around's no different than popping the hard stuff. He told me to mind my own business. I keep telling him to stay home and take care of the missus and the kids. So he says quit the BS. I don't think he really can help himself. It's an obsession. He's got to be in control of anybody he meets. What's the psychological term? Compensating? Down deep though; I think he really cares for Lorelei."

Something Johnson said bothered me.

"What did you say about Gaines caring for his wife?"

"I made a general statement. Ya know. With Ron's reputation he probably couldn't get another job in the Park Service. I keep telling him to lighten up so that he has a better future in the Service and to take care of his wife." Johnson said.

I asked the deputy chief ranger how long Jennifer Marcus had been visiting Gaines' office. Johnson said several months.

"Did you ever discuss Miss Marcus with your buddy?" Johnson nodded negatively.

"Not specifically by name. I think I've told you everything. Maybe I said too much. I hope I can trust you," Johnson said.

"My momma always told us young-uns to tell the truth, be honest and do the right thing no matter how hard that might be. I took the early park boat to Manhattan Sunday morning and went to church services. I wanted to clear my head and get some direction from a Higher Authority. This was one of the toughest decisions I've had to make. I hope I did the right thing."

I told Johnson I respected his candor. I added that neither he nor the ranger who spoke to him would be implicated. We shook hands and he left.

I then called Sam Belmont and asked for an appointment.

Chapter 24

Belmont sensed trouble the minute we entered his office.

"Come on in, gentlemen. Glad you could come by this afternoon." He escorted us to a long oak table surrounded by matching chairs.

Torre accepted a ginger ale which Belmont removed from the refrigerator behind his desk. The superintendent placed the can on one of several cork coasters that were stacked in the center of the conference table. He sat quietly and stoically and offered no comment as I recounted my conversation with Johnson. I was careful not to identify the deputy chief ranger or the young man who visited his apartment. I sensed that the superintendent didn't want to believe what he was hearing. He knew, however, that as incredulous as it sounded, there was a measure of truth to what I told him. After I outlined our findings and theories, Belmont did respond.

"Why, gentlemen?" he asked.

We told him we didn't know.

"Perhaps Jennifer Marcus was looking for excitement. The ultimate experience. Having sex with another woman inside the Statue of Liberty. The thrill of doing something illegal. Flaunting authority. We ain't got no answers," Torre said.

Belmont asked if we had confronted Ms Marcus and we answered negatively.

"I assume you plan to do so as soon as possible?" he then asked.

"Eventually. We still have some loose ends to tie up, first," I said.

Torre said that was the reason for our meeting.

"What do you wish me to do at this point? I must keep the regional office informed. I've got Congressional inquiries up to my waist. That's not counting a concerned and anxious public or the reporters calling me, writing and faxing me daily with their concerns," Belmont added.

"It's been frightful, gentlemen. Totally frightful. Should I contact Ms Marcus or Mr. Gaines?" he asked.

"No Not yet," I said.

Let me remind you again, gentlemen. As I have repeatedly said in the past, our Boston and Washington offices must hear it from me before they read anything in the press. Do you understand?"

I told him that he could call the regional office.

"Just tell them that the case is close to being solved. Do not implicate anyone at this point. Say we have kept you up-to-date on the latest developments and that we are confident that the case will be resolved in a matter of days. Please say no more to anyone," I said.

"Why don't I call the regional director while you both are here so that you may personally hear what I have to tell him? In this way there will be no misunderstanding," Belmont countered.

The superintendent reached for the phone at the far end of the conference table and dialed the number. When the regional director's secretary put him on the line, Belmont outlined generally what we discussed and urged the regional director to say nothing at this point. He then cupped his hand over the receiver and turned to me.

"May the regional director notify Washington?" he whispered.

I nodded affirmatively, repeating my stipulation that no further information be divulged. Belmont relayed this to the regional director. From the tone of the phone conversation, I sensed an agreement that whatever information was being shared would be held in strictest confidence.

"Anything else gentlemen?" Belmont asked. I nodded.

"Before you leave. Please bear with me for a few moments. You know that this comes as a terrible personal shock to me. It is inexplicable. It is out of character and totally incomprehensible. I can't believe it. Ronald Gaines and Jennifer Marcus. Two young people with wonderful careers ahead of them. What a tragedy. It is preposterous. I am in a state of shock."

With that he accompanied us out of his office and bid farewell.

On our way down to the first floor, I told Torre that we had little time to waste and suggested we call in Marcus and Gaines as quickly as possible.

"We have to make our move, Vin," I said.

We then retraced our steps and returned to Sam Belmont's office. His secretary accompanied us inside.

"Please call Ron Gaines and Miss Marcus. Once we're all together we will confront them with the facts. The information and evidence are hard to deny. We must advise them that they are primary suspects," I said.

Chapter 25

The phone awakened me. I looked at the digital face of my clock radio. It was two-twenty in the morning. I looked around. My wife was still asleep. "Thank God," I whispered. I picked up the receiver and waited.

"Lieutenant? Hey, I'm sorry to bother you. This is Officer Knox at Park Police headquarters."

"Yeah, Larry. What's up?" I asked. I rubbed my eyes with my left hand.

"Like I said, I'm sorry to bother you. I got a call five minutes ago from the superintendent at Liberty Island. Said it was extremely urgent and that he has to speak to you immediately," the dispatcher said.

"I'll call you right back," I said.

I walked to the bathroom and washed my face with cold water. I then went into the kitchen and dialed the dispatcher's number.

"Did Belmont say what it was about?" I asked.

"He wouldn't tell me. He said it was extremely urgent that he speak with you right away. Refused to tell me what it was in reference to," Knox said.

"Oh yes. He did say it may be a matter of life or death."

I grabbed a pencil and pad and jotted down the superintendent's home phone number. Then I opened the refrigerator and poured myself a glass of orange juice from a plastic container. I drank three quarters of the glass, placed it onto the kitchen counter, and dialed Belmont's number. My wife, who heard the phone ring and saw the light on in the kitchen, came into the room and sat down at the table opposite me. What a beautiful woman I married, I remember thinking. Even without makeup and at two-thirty in the morning.

Belmont picked up the phone after the first ring.

"Belmont here," he said.

"Sam. This is Mike Finnegan. You made an urgent call to my office. Something about life and death?"

"It *is* important, Michael. I'm terribly sorry I had you called at this ungodly hour. The Liberty Island dispatcher received a call within the last thirty or forty-five minutes from Mrs. Beverly Marcus, Jennifer's mother, in Alabama. She left her number and I called her back."

I was now fully awake.

"Mrs. Marcus said her daughter called her to say that she was in serious trouble. She admitted being infatuated with her boss and with a woman with whom she was having relations sporadically. Someone she met in New York City. She thinks she contributed to the woman's death. She swore to her mother that she didn't do anything to cause her any harm."

"Go on, Sam," I interrupted. I wanted him to know that I was still listening.

"She told her mother. Oh wait a moment please, Michael. I've got to get my glasses so I can decipher my notes. I wrote down the conversation exactly as it transpired. One moment please."

The delay seemed like an eternity. My blood boiled in anticipation. Finally Belmont returned.

"Are you still there, Michael? Good. Here it is exactly as Mrs. Marcus told me. 'I tried to do a favor for someone but it backfired. He let me down and now I've got a dead woman on my conscience.'"

"Did Jennifer identify the other person?" I asked Belmont.

"Apparently not. But from what Jennifer's mother told me, there was panic in the tone of her daughter's voice. She said she urged her daughter to do nothing rash. The family was totally behind her; was totally supportive. Mrs. Marcus told her daughter to speak with me in the morning and to ask for a leave of absence and then arrange to fly home as quickly as possible."

"Then Mrs. Marcus immediately called Liberty Island and asked the dispatcher to get in touch with you, Sam. Is that correct?" I asked.

"Correct, Michael. Mrs. Marcus called the dispatcher. He said he was not authorized under the federal privacy act to give out my home phone number but he called me. I called her back immediately. I then called the dispatcher to contact you."

I excused myself and gulped another glass of juice. My throat choked up and I desperately needed something to drink.

"There is more," the superintendent said.

"Jennifer Marcus said she was depressed and intended to take her own life. She kept referring to the fact that *he* let her down."

I asked Belmont if Jennifer told her mother what she intended to do.

"No. Mrs. Marcus tried to keep Jennifer on the phone to convince her to come home. I told you Mrs. Marcus urged her daughter to put in for an extended leave of absence and get help in Alabama. In fact, Mrs. Marcus said she would call Jennifer's father and they would fly to New York on the first available flight to be with Jennifer during this crisis. I believe Mrs. Marcus said she and Jennifer's father were divorced."

"How did Ms Marcus respond?"

"According to her mother, Jennifer said that would not be necessary. It would be better if she tried to resolve the situation without her parents' intervention. She just wanted her family to know about her depression. Maybe she was cleansing her soul."

"You're absolutely sure she didn't say or give a clue as to who the *he* might be that she referred to?" I asked again.

"No," Belmont responded. The superintendent said he immediately called Ron Gaines and asked if he knew where Ms Marcus lived so that New York City police could be notified. "I don't have access to personal files at home. Gaines claimed he didn't have her address so he called the dispatch office for her home phone number. With that information he tried to call Jennifer's apartment but got no response."

"We must find her, Michael. It may be a matter of life or death."

"Did she carry her service revolver when off duty?"

"All weapons must be secured at the end of each shift. That's the policy. The only exceptions are Gaines and William Johnson. I have no way of knowing whether she had her revolver with her," Belmont added.

I told the superintendent to wait by the phone while I called Detective Torre. Then I called Manhattan South and had them call the sergeant at home.

"It's an emergency. Please have Torre call me immediately," I gave the dispatcher my home phone number. Within minutes the phone rang and I grabbed for the receiver after one ring.

"Vin?"

"No, Michael. It's Sam Belmont again. I prevailed upon the dispatcher to give me your number. We found Ms Marcus' revolver. It was on the floor of the second level of the Statue of Liberty."

"What in Hell are you talking about, Sam?" I felt my heart racing. Sensing my anguish, my wife got up, walked behind me, and rubbed my shoulders.

"It was lying on the floor next to her body."

"Sam! Whose body?"

"Jennifer Marcus."

"That's about the worst news—"

"Yes, Michael. Ms Marcus shot herself in the temple with her service revolver at the approximate location where Ms Konowitz' body was discovered."

I remained seated, trembling. My mouth was wide open.

"Michael! Michael! Are you all right?"

My wife overheard Belmont's voice. She released my shoulders, put her hand to her mouth and ran crying from the kitchen.

"William Johnson quickly dressed and ran to the dispatch office from his apartment. With the assistance of other rangers he was able to break open Ms Marcus' locker. When they found the service revolver missing, Johnson ordered the rangers to thoroughly search the monument and the island to ascertain that she was not there.

"Michael. I am devastated. I am in a complete state of shock. It is like losing a daughter. I feel terrible."

I told Belmont to order the monument closed until detectives got there and to notify the regional office. I repeated my initial directives when Ms Konowitz' body was found, and told Belmont to keep everyone on the island until we arrived.

"No one is allowed inside the monument. That includes Gaines, Johnson and even you Sam. It's for your own good. I don't want to find your fingerprints anywhere in the statue. I don't want anything disturbed."

"I will notify the regional director and Ron Gaines," Belmont said.

"I'll have Torre contact the medical examiner's office. Have someone meet our boats when we get there. I'll be there as soon as I can. I think Sergeant Torre will want to be there too."

I told the superintendent not to discuss any part of his conversation with Mrs. Marcus. I added that I would notify Mel Davis and that all phone calls should be directed to him as the official spokesman from this time forward.

"And remember, Sam. No one. Not you, Gaines or Johnson is to go inside the Statue of Liberty. Do I make myself clear? Do you understand?"

I replaced the receiver onto its cradle. I retrieved the unfinished glass of orange juice but could not drink it. My hand shook. My stomach churned. And I shivered.

"Good old Sam Belmont. Always the consummate gentlemen, even under the most adverse conditions," I told my wife after I returned to the bedroom. The phone interrupted my thought process. It was Vince Torre. I explained my conversation with Belmont and we agreed to meet at the Park Police dock within two hours.

Unbeknownst to me, while I was speaking to Torre, William Johnson was dialing Ron Gaines' number.

Chapter 26

The park vessel from Ellis Island pulled into the ferry dock at Liberty Island. Before the deckhand could secure the vessel to its moorings, Gaines jumped ashore and ran toward the administration building as surprised rangers looked on. Without talking to anyone, he barged into the conference room where Torre and I were meeting with Sam Belmont and William Johnson.

We looked up but said nothing. Finally Belmont invited Gaines to join us. Belmont then told the chief ranger that detectives were inside the Statue of Liberty. Gaines remained silent. This was quite a contrast to our confrontation when Ms Konowitz' body was found.

When the superintendent finished outlining what had transpired earlier in the morning, I asked if anyone had an idea who the *he* was that Ms Marcus told her mother about. I looked at Gaines who sat silently as if meditating.

Torre than removed his memo pad from his jacket pocket and leafed quickly through the pages until he came to what he was looking for.

"Immediately after we found the first body, Lieutenant Finnegan and I and our staffs interviewed each ranger who was on duty the night before. Because of their backgrounds and what we could piece together, we felt that there were several possible suspects. Let me tell you what we know." He looked at his pad.

"We had reason to believe Miss Marcus was a primary suspect but we couldn't be certain. She became belligerent when I asked her whether she had many woman friends. This was a routine question but she was insulted. She had no way of knowing that Johnson would detail her to open the Statue that morning. Is that correct?"

Johnson nodded affirmatively.

"If she was involved in the woman's death, she needed help," Torre added.

Torre went down the list of possible suspects. I was surprised he was so candid in front of Gaines and Johnson. On the other hand, I trusted his judgment.

"Varga...Divorced. His wife took off with another man so he claims to hate women. Can't afford to date because of his low pay and the high cost of living in New York. Wants outta New York desperately. Says he feels sorry for the dead woman but asks what in Hell she was doing at the Statue after the island closed. Would he kill a woman to get even with his ex-wife?"

No one said anything.

"Then there was Chadwicke. Nice young man. Also divorced. Happy go lucky. Could've been seekin' the thrill of doing somethin' different, such as screwin' a woman inside the Statue. Said he was a standup comic in a club a coupla nights a week and meets women there. Who knows?"

The detective then outlined our interviews with the other rangers, all of whom exhibited potential motives. He looked at Gaines and without missing a beat told the chief ranger that he was a suspect as well.

"Wouldn't that've been somethin' else if we let you investigate a Goddamned murder that we suspected you of being involved in?" No one in the room smiled. Gaines stirred briefly in his chair. A troubled smile crossed his face.

I mentioned that Torre forgot Skip Brandwyne.

"Oh yeah. That guy." Torre then summarized our interview.

Suddenly Torre shot a glance back at the chief ranger.

"How well did you know Ms Marcus?" he asked.

"She worked for me. I knew her as well as any of the rangers. They're always welcome to meet with me to discuss a problem, regulations or whatever else they want to talk about." Looking toward his deputy, he said that his and Johnson's doors are always open to staff.

"That's right, isn't it Will?"

"Absolutely," the deputy ranger said.

"Did you have any dealings with her above and beyond your supervisor-employee relationship?" Torre asked, his eyes narrowing.

"I'm a happily married man, sergeant. Why would I be involved with a woman at least ten years my junior? I'd be out of my cotton-picking mind, don't you think? I have a mind to report you to your supervisor when this investigation is closed."

Still the same arrogant bastard, I thought.

"Sergeant Torre asked you a simple question. How well did you know Jennifer Marcus professionally and socially? Calm down and answer the question," I responded.

Gaines' elbows rested on the table, his fingers entwined tightly.

"We did get together from time-to-time to discuss job-related issues. That's all," Gaines said.

"Where?" I asked.

"In my office. Maybe once in awhile we'd go off the island for a quick sandwich or a pizza and beer."

"Is this your common practice when rangers need help or advice in solving a problem?" I asked.

"I try to be available to any rangers who want my help. If it's a personal issue that can't or shouldn't be discussed in the office or on Liberty Island, I see nothing wrong with getting together for a bite to eat. That's harmless," Gaines stammered.

"That's not the way we understand it," Torre countered.

"What do you mean? I don't know what you're talking about, sergeant," Gaines spit.

"Don't play games with us, Mr. Gaines. You're one tough son of a bitch. One can shave by the shine on your shoes. You abide one hundred percent by the rules and regulations. You're not known to socialize. You no doubt are aware of regulations concerning fraternization. But just a few seconds ago you told us you went out with Ms Marcus for a sandwich in Manhattan. To discuss park business, of course," Torre persisted.

Gaines sat still. His face turned crimson but he remained silent.

"Let me repeat the question, Mr. Gaines. How well didja know Ms Marcus?" Torre asked again.

"I told you," Gaines said.

"When we left the crime scene a couple of weeks ago, you ran ahead of us to your office to change into your civilian clothes."

"So what? Is that a crime? Show me where I violated the regulations by changing into a pair of jeans and calling me wife to tell her I'd be home late so she wouldn't worry."

"How do you generally get home from Liberty Island?" I asked the chief ranger.

"The park boat takes me to Ellis Island. From there I drive over the temporary bridge to Jersey City and down the Turnpike. What does that have to do with the investigation and Jennifer's, I mean Ms Marcus's death?"

"When we got back to Manhattan, you were on the launch with us. You walked toward the subway. That sure is the long way home to New Jersey, isn't it?" I said.

Gaines said nothing.

"You took the subway somewhere didn't ya?" Torre asked.

"I don't recall," Gaines whispered.

"Come on now. You don't expect us to believe that," Torre said.

"I…I…I was going to visit a friend in Midtown Manhattan," Gaines stammered.

"Who was that friend, Gaines?" Torre asked.

"Ron. Be truthful. There's nothing to be gained by not telling the truth. For the good of all of us including you, please be straightforward with us. Were you intimate with Jennifer Marcus?" It was the soothing tone of reason from Superintendent Belmont.

Gaines was deflated. He stared into space as if seeking Divine guidance.

"So what of it? I was going to visit Jennifer Marcus at her apartment. I didn't commit any crime. He removed his eyeglasses and wiped sweat from his forehead and lenses. This was a nervous habit I noticed earlier.

"So you went to Jennifer Marcus' apartment. How frequently did you visit her?"

"It's none of your business. I don't see where this has any relevance to the murder and suicide investigations. What I do after hours is my own fucking business."

"That may be up to a court of law to determine," I warned him.

"Right now, your ass is on thin ice. We're hopeful that your answers will get us through this madness…Now, how frequently?"

"I met with her whenever she needed to talk to me. You know she was a fragile person and it had a serious effect on her when she found the body lying there in the Statue of Liberty. You can check the records. Call the personnel office and find out how many hours she took off to get away from the island. Yes. We met in my office and in her apartment whenever she needed someone to confide in. She felt that although she had nothing to do with the death of Ms Konowitz she was considered suspect numero uno. In fact, just a few days ago, she came to my office during the day and cried to me that everywhere she went people were staring at her and thinking of her as a murderess. Her mind was playing tricks with her. Yeah. I met with her. That's the side of me you guys never saw. I'm a bastard when it comes to rules and regulations and I know my reputation is shit in the Park Service. But there's another side of Ron Gaines you never saw. And yes, we were intimate, as the superintendent put it. Only Will Johnson here knows me for what I am." He looked at his deputy.

"Go ahead and tell them, Will. Tell 'em about the lack of discipline on the island when I got here and how I had to shape up the troops."

Johnson said nothing.

"I tried being the nice guy but those bastards'll step all over you if you let them. I had no choice but to be the hard-ass and keep everyone in line. Did I see Jennifer Marcus in our off-hours? Bet your life I did and I'm glad of it." He again wiped his glasses.

"But I love my wife and children and I'll be damned if I will let anything or anyone come between us. My relationship with Jennifer Marcus started innocently. It led in a direction I didn't want it to go in. How do you avoid those things? You read and hear stories like this every day and think it will never happen to you. However, there's nothing I can do about it now except get on with my life and try to put that episode behind me."

"At any time during your visits with her in your office or in her apartment or over lunch, did she ever mention a woman she was close to or wanted to bring to the island?" I asked.

The chief ranger again wiped his forehead.

"Please. For heavens sakes, answer the question," Belmont told him. The exchange clearly bewildered Johnson. He removed a thin government-issue memo pad and pencil from his shirt pocket and jotted a short note. He ripped the page from the pad, folded it in half, and pushed it across the table toward me. I read it quickly and put it into my pocket.

"At any time to the best of your recollection did Jennifer ever tell you about setting up a blind date on the island for one of your rangers?" I asked.

"In what context? We discussed a lot of issues," Gaines said.

"Oh, I don't know specifically. To help a buddy who wanted to meet a woman but didn't feel comfortable initiating a date, perhaps," I said.

"Again, I don't know what relevance this has to the investigation, lieutenant," Gaines responded.

"We have reason to believe that someone overheard a phone

conversation between Ms Marcus and an unidentified person. This was reported to park authorities. It may have some bearing on Ms Konowitz' murder," I said.

"When did this so-called phone conversation take place?" the chief ranger asked.

"Several days before the body was found," I said.

"I know nothing about a blind date," Gaines answered.

We had no more questions. Sam Belmont asked if he could talk to us privately, however.

"As far as we know, Gaines was at home with his wife and children when the body was discovered," Belmont reminded us.

I reminded Belmont that he admitted having a relationship with Jennifer Marcus.

"Therefore, Gaines certainly knew what was happening. I can't believe that during some of their more intimate moments, as you described it, Sam, she didn't confide in him; tell him what was on her mind."

"Could other rangers have been involved, lieutenant? Such a diverse group of men and women. That is hard to fathom, I must say," he interjected.

"That's not what we're saying," Torre emphasized.

"Let me continue. Jennifer Marcus had a sexual inclination for both men and women. We've established that she knew Ms Konowitz and, in fact, have reason to believe that she was carrying on an intimate relationship with her. We have no concrete evidence and do not know the frequency. But there are witnesses who have seen them together. That has been established during our investigation." Belmont sat quietly.

Chapter 27

I called Birmingham, Alabama and arranged to fly down to meet Jennifer Marcus' mother. She met me at the airport and drove me to her home. Over coffee, she asked me about the investigation and about the dead woman.

"We were hoping to question your daughter further. We believe that she was friendly with the deceased. She probably was withholding information."

"Do you mean, lieutenant, that she may have contributed to the woman's death?"

"We don't know for sure. Your daughter's suicide was a major setback."

I asked Mrs. Marcus about Jennifer's childhood. She contributed little new information.

"Please don't be offended. But I must ask about your daughter's sexual orientation."

Mrs. Marcus lifted her coffee cup to her lips. She slowly nursed its contents.

"Please be specific," she said. I sensed she was stalling, not wanting to answer my question."

"Did she ever display tendencies toward other women or discuss her adult friends?"

"To the contrary. Jennifer had many male friends. She dated quite a bit in high school and college. She was very pretty and intelligent. She also did have a wonderful sense of humor. Although I hesitate to admit it, she displayed many of her father's traits. She was in a college sorority where she had many women friends as well. To the best of my knowledge, all her friends were…How shall I say it? Normal. But then I did not see Jennifer that frequently once she went to New York to live. I wasn't too happy about that although Jennifer refused to listen to me. You know how young people are today, lieutenant. Is it possible she may have picked up those so-called lesbian tendencies that you mentioned from someone in New York City? Please do not take me personally, Mr. Finnegan. I just do not trust those New Yorkers. They are too brazen and pushy. To answer your question, though, Jennifer to the best of my knowledge did not show or display any sexual tendencies towards women while here or in college. I would know if she had. Who would know her better than her own mother? Again. In answer to your question. I cannot recall anything abnormal about my late daughter's behavior. I'm terribly sorry that I cannot help you."

"Did she ever mention a specific friend in New York?"

"No. She didn't…Wait…"

Mrs. Marcus paused again. She took another sip from her coffee cup. She asked if she could pour a second cup for me and I accepted. She continued when she returned from the kitchen.

"Jennifer never mentioned his name. She said she was concerned about a co-worker. One of the other rangers. She never elaborated."

"How long ago was that?"

"I'd say several months ago. Jennifer and I usually spoke once a week. She was elated that she was able to help him with a problem. Oh yes. It's coming back now. I asked if she had a crush on the young man."

"What was Jennifer's response?"

"She said she was too smart to develop a relationship with a casual acquaintance. Especially someone she worked with. She said that this young man was a co-worker and no more."

"You said she volunteered to help the young man. Did she say if anyone asked her? If so, did she identify that person?"

"My daughter was very closed-mouthed like her father. She always confided in me. But in general terms."

"Did Jennifer ever mention Ron Gaines?"

"Yes. Her boss."

I sipped my coffee.

"Why do you ask?"

"We think Mr. Gaines and your daughter were having an affair.

"That's impossible, Lieutenant Finnegan. Jennifer always referred to Mr. Gaines as impossible to work for. When she was home last Christmas, in fact, she said she considered requesting a transfer. She couldn't work for him any longer."

"Was your daughter strong-willed?" I asked.

"She knew what she wanted. I keep referring to my ex-husband. Please excuse me. But he is the father to my children. She inherited her father's genes. Jennifer could be assertive."

"It is possible Ron Gaines used your daughter. He visited your daughter's apartment frequently."

"But he is a married man. My daughter told me that he had pictures of his children in his office. And yes, he had the most attractive wife. Her photograph is on his desk."

"It happens every day. Older men fall for younger women."

"Your daughter, Mrs. Marcus, was intelligent and attractive. It could be that Gaines was undergoing midlife crisis."

"If as you say, lieutenant, that my daughter was involved in any way with the dead woman, she was forced into the situation. Jennifer would not have intentionally done anything that would result in harm to another individual. My daughter was very kind and gentle and had a love of life. Someone may have manipulated her. I'm sure that my daughter was intimidated. Maybe that's why she wanted a transfer."

"Are you certain, Mrs. Marcus, that your daughter never told you who asked her to fix up a ranger with a date?"

"Absolutely. I would have remembered had she told me, lieutenant. I believe I have told you everything I know."

"Does the name William Johnson mean anything, Mrs. Marcus?"

"Yes."

"How?"

"My daughter was fond of Mr. Johnson. She spoke highly of him. In fact, she mentioned a few months ago that she wished he was the boss and not Mr. Gaines."

"Did she ever mention Mr. Johnson in a social context?"

"Are you implying, Mr. Finnegan, that she may have been intimate with him? You know, of course, that he is an African-American. She would never dream of doing something such as that."

I told Mrs. Marcus that it was not a sexual connotation I had in mind. She asked me to explain.

"Did your daughter ever mention having personal conversations with Mr. Johnson? Asking him for advice on how to deal with Mr. Gaines? Do you know whether Jennifer asked Mr. Johnson to intercede in her behalf? Did she ask Mr. Johnson to help her achieve the transfer she sought?"

"No, Mr. Finnigan. Her references to Mr. Johnson were always general in nature. Jennifer was tight-lipped when it came to her personal affairs. Her mention of Mr. Johnson was in passing reference."

After lunch, Mrs. Marcus showed me through the house and drove me back to the airport. I tried napping on the plane but couldn't. I was bothered by too many gnawing questions. Why did Jennifer tell her mother she wanted to change jobs? Was this an excuse to leave New York, a love affair that had gone sour, and memories of a murder? Did she have a love-hate relationship with Ron Gaines? Was Jennifer a victim or a perpetrator? Was she lesbian or straight? Did she never tell her mother about her possible relationship with William Johnson beyond the workplace? Was her mom an overbearing parent who was hiding embarrassing information from me?

These questions, I felt, needed to be answered if we were to solve the homicide investigation.

Chapter 28

A major break came in late October and from an unexpected source. After spending three hours in bed unable to sleep and staring at a dark ceiling, my wife tapped me on the shoulder. My illuminated digital alarm read one forty-eight.

"You up?" she whispered.

"Yeah. Why?"

"I was thinking."

"That can be dangerous at this time of day," I answered sarcastically.

"Listen. You know that young ranger you told me about who overheard Jennifer Marcus on the phone?"

"The shy one who wants out of the Park Service?" I asked.

"Yes. You said his father and grandfather were in the Park Service. That would make his father about the same age as Sam Belmont."

I silently pondered Marge's suggestion.

"Michael. Are you listening to me?"

"What do you think I'm doing? Playing solitaire?"

"You don't have to be so sarcastic. That's the second time since I tapped you on the shoulder. You're laughing at me and I don't like it. I'm trying to help you. Act more civil and hear me out. It's the least you can do." Marge rested her head on her pillow and began to cry. I reached over and pulled her close to me. Damnit, I thought. Why does she always make me feel like a heel?"

She slowly regained her composure.

"Is it possible that the kid's father and the superintendent know each other? Maybe they worked in the same park somewhere in their careers."

"Where'd you get that crazy notion?" I asked.

"Why is it so crazy?"

"Because it is. That's why."

"It's simple. Listen Mike. The kid wants out. His father calls an old friend, the superintendent, and asks him to encourage the young man to stay. Wouldn't you do that for our kid if you had to? Remember when you got out of the Army and told your parents you wanted to join the Park Police? Your father did everything he could to get you to join the NYPD. But you made up your mind. You said you wanted to do *your* thing."

"You're telling me Sam Belmont had something to do with the murder? That's impossible," I said.

Marge snapped on the lamp on her night table and sat up. She was wearing a thin nightgown. She still had a great body, I thought.

"Hear me out. Belmont gets a call from the ranger's father. The superintendent thinks Brandwyne would stay in New York if he had a social life. He asks a woman on his staff to find the young man a date. Jennifer feels threatened and volunteers to do so. Probably out of fear of the superintendent. Something goes wrong and the woman dies."

"That's great. You've solved the murder. Now can we try to sleep?"

Marge sat up. Her hands rested on her hips.

"You're still laughing at me. You owe me an apology." I stared at her, trying to not laugh.

"You want me to believe at almost two in the morning that Sam Belmont and the kid's father conspired to keep a kid in the National Park Service against his free will? You've got to be kidding. For this you woke me. Can't it wait until the morning when we can discuss it more rationally?"

Then it hit me.

"Did my father have anything to do with this?"

"Why do you ask that? Don't you give me any credit for having a brain?" Marge asked.

"Dad put you up to this. Didn't he?"

"I don't know what you're talking about."

"He told you to suggest this to me. Admit it. Come clean."

Marge began to laugh.

"Yes. He did. But he didn't want you to know it. He wanted it to be my idea. Please don't get mad. You know he means well."

I laughed too.

"Your father is very proud of you, Michael. He's gotten over being hurt that you didn't join the Department. This theory about Belmont and the young man's father was *his* idea but he was embarrassed to mention it to you. He thought you would tell him to mind his own business. He made me swear I'd never let on. It took a lot of courage for him to help you like this."

I pondered what Marge had said. I knew she was right.

"Where did he come up with that theory.or does he know more than he told you?"

"He said it was just a hunch. I guess when you are a cop as long as he was, you'll develop those intuitions," Marge added.

"Why didn't he tell me himself?"

"I already told you. He was embarrassed. He didn't know how you would react. He just wanted to help you. Now I'm not going to let you sleep until you apologize or...I've got a better idea." Marge paused long enough for me to ask.

"Make love to me." She hugged me tightly. I responded.

Marge was up early. After making our breakfast, she stood in the doorway to the bathroom and watched me shave.

"You want me to follow your clues. So I go to the boss and say I've got the suspect. My wife and my father told me who did it." I chuckled.

"That's your job. You're the cop. Figure out how to do it," she said. Marge walked back into the kitchen. I detected a smile.

Chapter 29

My wife was right about one thing. It was my job. I did follow up on my father's idea.

Armed with a court order from a federal judge in Manhattan, I requisitioned copies of Sam Belmont's and Leo Brandwyne Sr.'s employment records from the Office of Personnel Management in Virginia. They showed that Belmont and Brandwyne did, in fact, work together in the 80s in California. After securing copies of Brandwyne's telephone records from the previous year, I overnight mailed records of our investigation to our San Francisco Field Office, asking that they assign a detective to interview Skip Brandwyne's father. An interview with Sam Belmont was next on my agenda.

"I'm still getting a lot of pressure. Where are we on the investigation?" Belmont asked as soon as I walked into his office.

"We're almost ready to make an arrest," I said.

Belmont firmly grabbed my right hand and began shaking it He draped his left arm over my shoulder.

"Wonderful news. I can't wait to inform the regional director. When may I do so?" he asked. Belmont placed two cans of ginger ale on the conference table and sat down. I sat opposite him.

"How well do you know Leo Brandwyne Sr.?" I asked. I detected Belmont's hesitation.

"How or why would I know Leo Brandwyne?" Belmont responded unconvincingly.

"You're not answering my question, Sam. Let me rephrase it. When did you last speak to Leo Brandwyne Sr.?"

"I don't see the need for this line of questioning."

"You received a call in December from Leo. He asked you to encourage his son to stay in the Park Service."

"That's a lie." Belmont flushed.

I opened my briefcase and handed the superintendent a copy of Brandwyne's phone records. Two calls to Belmont were circled with a red marker.

Belmont nursed his soda. After a pause, he responded.

"Oh yes. I remember. Since when is it a crime for a concerned father to communicate with his son's boss about an issue of mutual concern?"

"What was the mutual concern? I asked.

"Mr. Brandwyne wanted me to do what I could to keep his son in the Park Service. He thought I would have more influence on the young man than he had. I have always maintained a strong desire to see young men and women with career potential remain in the system. I fail to see anything wrong with that. To the contrary. I believe that is admirable."

I handed him his personnel file and a copy of the court order.

The superintendent turned ashen.

I read Belmont his Miranda rights and asked about the phone calls. He reiterated that Brandwyne was concerned about his son.

"How did you respond?"

"I said I would talk to Skip."

"Did you offer to help find the young man a woman?"

"I told Leo I was uncomfortable. I would make some discreet inquiries. I couldn't do more."

"Did you?"

"Yes. In general terms with Ms Marcus. I didn't identify young Mr.

Brandwyne. I asked what she would do if a friend was about to forfeit a promising career because of loneliness."

"Did she offer to help?" I asked.

"She demanded to know who she would be helping. I told her. I had no choice."

"Was she intimidated?"

"Perhaps. She did assure me that if she did help, she would not embarrass Brandwyne or me. I had some reservations. I feared…"

"Blackmail?" I interrupted. "Leo Brandwyne could have squeezed you. Jennifer Marcus could have pressured you for a promotion or something else."

"Are you implying she would have asked me for sex?"

"I didn't bring it up, Sam. You did."

Belmont slumped backward, contemplating his response.

"What would you expect me to do? Leo and I have been friends for many years."

"Did he threaten you?" I asked.

"Absolutely not. Don't you understand? I tried to help a long-time friend and prevent the Park Service from losing a good employee. I had no ulterior motive. Believe me."

"Do you think Ms Marcus discussed your request with her lover?"

"Gaines?"

"Was there someone else?"

"Not that I am aware of."

"Did you and Ms Marcus discuss Brandwyne after your initial conversation?"

"No."

"Do you think Gaines would use this against you?"

"How could he?"

"Pressure you into doing something you do not wish to do. Get him a transfer. Testify for him if his wife files for divorce. Demand payment for keeping his mouth shut."

I got up to leave.

"Don't do anything rash, Sam," I said.
"Why would I?"
"*You* answer that one," I said.

CHAPTER 30

The administrative officer where Sam Belmont and Leo Brandwyne worked together e-mailed me the retirement address of their former superintendent. I called Max Gomes in a Raleigh, North Carolina suburb.

"I haven't spoken to those two since they left California. I've followed Sam's career, though. The Park Service is like a family. You know what your employees and colleagues are doing. We've got a Helluva alumni association and network," he said.

I asked him about his former staff persons.

"Belmont was a ranger. He had a law enforcement commission. Tough hombre. Mean and lean. Stretched the regs to the maximum. Let me give you some examples," he volunteered.

"We suspected Sam was profiling female drivers with out-of-state license plates. He'd find some infraction. Loud muffler disturbing the resource. Garbage can not tightly shut. Gum wrapper near the campsite."

"Why didn't you do something?"

"Couldn't document it. Couldn't penalize him on hearsay. By the time we got around to investigating the incidents and complaints, the campers were already gone or too intimidated to say anything. Now that you mention it; I recall there was a distinct pattern. Most of the citations were issued on the last day of the permit. The visitors would send in a check for the fine rather than come back and appeal the citation before a federal magistrate. No formal complaints so I couldn't do anything."

"Any complaints of a sexual nature?"

"A family from Milwaukee accused Belmont of harassing their teenaged daughter. When I asked for something in writing they refused."

"What did you do?"

"I told Belmont I wanted his resignation or a request for transfer. He decided to leave the park."

"How did he become superintendent of the Statue of Liberty?"

"He moved east to Washington, D. C. Married a woman on the staff of an influential Congressman on the House Natural Resources Committee. She prevailed upon her boss to use his influence."

I asked about Leo Brandwyne.

"They fought like Hell. Brandwyne was in maintenance. Lived by the book. You know, the Code of Federal Regulations. Was religious but had a bad temper. It didn't take much to set him off. He thought he was doing the Lord's duty by protecting the resource. Anyone who damaged the resource was a sinner. Don't know what happened to him. Haven't heard his name in years."

I asked Gomes for specifics.

"Leo was red carded. That means he was trained to fight forest fires. While he was detailed to fight a blaze in Idaho, Belmont raped his wife. Sam denied it. Leo's wife refused to sign an affidavit. She was afraid of her husband."

"Did they have children?"

"Sam and Pat had no kids. I think Brandwyne had the one son, Leo Jr."

"Did Leo find out about the rape?"

"He knew about it. People thought Leo was a dumb rube. Dontcha believe it. Leo was a slick son of a bitch. He knew everything. Collected favors from some pretty high up people."

I interviewed several other superintendents by phone. They generally substantiated what Gomes told me. A pattern emerged.

Chapter 31

When Torre and I returned to Belmont's office several days later, he appeared tired.

"I'm sorry, gentlemen. I've not slept very well lately," he said. Belmont ushered us to the upholstered chairs in front of his desk.

"You're not telling us everything. I think you're withholding information," Torre said.

"You can't be accusing me of being an accessory to the murder, sergeant," Belmont responded.

"Did Mr. Brandwyne call to threaten you?"

"Why would he do that?"

"On accounta you raped his wife. He never forgot or forgave. Some people hold grudges a long time."

Belmont reached toward a lower drawer of his desk. Torre and I instinctively grabbed for our holsters.

"Relax, gentlemen," Belmont said, holding a bottle of bourbon and pouring it into a plastic cup.

"I'd offer you both a drink. That would constitute a bribe. Wouldn't it?" he sneered.

Torre flushed with anger. He desperately tried to maintain his cool.

"I've been a cop a long time. I've gotten guys to talk when other cops got shit. I ain't much on psychology crap. But I get what I want. I ain't getting what I want now and you're pissing me off. What didn't you tell Lieutenant Finnegan? It's gonna be tough patrolling a lonely park in the middle of the night in Juneau if you don't talk. Now who in Hell killed Shirley Konowitz?" Torre demanded.

Belmont downed the bourbon and stared silently at the empty cup. He refilled it.

"Look, Sam," I interjected.

"Sergeant Torre and I know you wanted to help Skip Brandwyne. But you've got a stack of letters from school kids who are afraid to come to Liberty Island and you've got the regional director and Congressmen on your case. The longer you stall, the harder it's going to be on you."

"Will it be used against me?" Belmont whispered.

"It's up to the federal magistrate. We'll try to go to bat. I can't make any promises beyond that."

"Maybe retirement with a clean record?"

"You heard me, Sam."

The superintendent pushed his cup to one side.

"Leo and I worked together out west. I was a ranger out of college, wanting to make a name. He and I had nothing in common. He wasn't educated. Don't even know if Leo ever graduated from high school. Never saw a guy with his street smarts though. He was handy as Hell. Could fix anything and everything and he did. He even fixed things for people in town outside the park."

Belmont grabbed the cup and threw back its contents, refilling it a third time.

"Our philosophies were different completely. He was into religion. One of those born-agains. We liked each other although we argued frequently. Don't ask me to explain. Despite their differences, our wives got along too. My wife Pat couldn't have children. Leo Jr. was like our son."

The superintendent excused himself and staggered toward the small bathroom adjoining his office. We again reached for our holsters in anticipation of trouble. Hearing the toilet flush, we relaxed. Belmont returned.

"Never fails. Bourbon does that to me all the time," he smiled.

"Where were we? Oh yes. We lived in government housing inside the park. Our home was next to the Brandwynes. Leo's wife was gorgeous. Thin waist and big bust. And she had beautiful long legs. I loved her southern drawl. My wife had a job as a secretary in town hall and left my lunch in the refrigerator. One day I drove home and there she was. Leo's wife was wearing a bikini and lying on a chaise lounge in their yard. Leo was in Idaho so she invited me in for a drink. She then pounced all over me before I could close the damn door. Kept crying she was lonely. Leo always out fixing and repairing things and doing favors for everyone. Fighting a forest fire in Idaho apparently pushed her over the edge. She was feeling sorry for herself and needed a man. She cried to me that Leo was always too tired or too busy to pay attention to her and their son. Good thing Skip was in school. She was like a pup in heat."

Belmont chuckled as he reached for his cup of bourbon.

"Next thing I knew, Leo was pissed off at me. Damnit. If he'd paid more attention to his wife she wouldn't need another man. Then the superintendent called me into his office and gave me a verbal lashing. He threatened to have me terminated and brought up on charges. But Leo's wife admitted she initiated it and charges were dropped. We agreed I should leave the park for a new assignment."

"Did Brandwyne ever threaten you?" I asked.

"Don't recall. We left a couple of months later. By then we were talking to each other. The night before we moved, Leo called me over and showed me the biggest damned Rolodex I'd ever seen. It was filled with handwritten notes and business cards. From politicians, Park Service people, complete strangers. Some of the names were from out of state."

"How did he cultivate the list?" Torre asked.

"I told you before. Don't let Leo's lack of a formal education fool you. He's savvy. Street smart. He had access to government equipment and supplies and knew how to use them. Probably didn't pay for half the stuff he had in his workshop. Probably paid for by the taxpayers," Belmont chuckled.

"When something needed fixing, call Leo. If the guy was important, Leo didn't charge. He accumulated chits that way." Belmont rose from his desk. He was unsteady and nearly tripped. He staggered to a wall where he leaned, his arms crossed in front of him.

"One time we drove into town for drinks. Just Leo and me. We got stone drunk and tried to drive home. A rookie cop, maybe on the force a few weeks, stops and writes us a ticket for drunk driving. The next day the chief calls to apologize. The ticket was quashed. Leo told me he fixed the chief's wife washing machine and refused money. He said he was bedding her on the side. And the chief didn't know about it." Belmont laughed.

"You said Leo was a religious man."

Belmont snickered but said nothing.

Torre was restless. He toyed with his Zippo.

"Go ahead. Light up. See if I care," Belmont told him.

Torre reached in his shirt pocket for a cigarette. He lit it.

"Who killed Shirley Konowitz?" he asked.

Belmont staggered back to his desk. His elbows rested on a stack of papers. He stared through bloodshot eyes at the bourbon cup that he gripped tightly at eye level. There was a long pause.

"Leo Junior."

Torre and I stared at each other.

"Repeat that, Sam," I whispered.

"I just told you. Leo's kid. My godson. My friend's boy. He killed that woman."

"Who told you?" I asked.

The superintendent sat mute. He stared into space as if in a hypnotic trance. Placing the half-empty bourbon cup on his desk, he crossed his fingers to form an arch. His elbows rested on the desk. We waited for Sam Belmont to continue.

"Jenfer...Jenfer...Jen-ni-fer told me," he mumbled incoherently, trying desperately to pronounce her name correctly.

Again Torre and I glanced at each other.

"You appear to be shocked. Jennifer and I were alone in her apartment." At least he pronounced her name correctly, I thought.

"What were you doing in her apartment and when was this?" Torre shouted.

"It was about a month...Maybe five weeks after the body was found..." Belmont had regained control of his speech and appeared more composed.

"Miss Marcus...Jennifer...was able to secure my private telephone number here at the office. I don't know who gave it to her since the only ones familiar with the number are my secretary and my wife. Of course the regional director. Not even Gaines or Johnson have that number."

Belmont took another sip from the cup. He steadied his voice.

"She said she had to see me right away. She said she was desperate to talk to me."

"So what did you do?" I asked.

"I suggested she call my secretary and make an appointment. I was free any afternoon that week. But she didn't want anyone to know about her phone call. She asked if she could meet me away from the office. Perhaps in Manhattan for coffee."

"Did you accept her proposal?" I asked.

"Reluctantly. She was concerned that people considered her the primary suspect and that her career was ruined. She told me that her parents were divorced and that as a child she missed a father to talk to. He was always too busy in business to pay any attention to her."

When I asked about her mother, Belmont said Jennifer described her as a wonderful woman, but very neurotic and interfering. She said something about New York being too wild and not a good place for a young woman to be living alone in. I detected a slight smile on the superintendent's lips.

"We had a pleasant conversation and Jennifer asked if we could meet again. Away from the island. I hesitated. In fact, I emphasized that in the future she must go through normal channels. As I said before, go through my secretary. I couldn't be more emphatic. I told her that under no condition would I deviate from my policy."

I sensed that Belmont had drank himself sober. At least he acted as if he had. I asked what caused him to change his mind about meeting the ranger after hours.

"Jennifer called my secretary about a week later. She made an appointment to meet me here. She sat exactly where you are, sergeant," he said pointing to Torre.

She came to the office on her day off specifically to meet me. I remember exactly what she wore. It was chilly so she had a nylon zippered jacket on over a white blouse. She was wearing tight fitting slacks. She removed her jacket and stood as she draped her jacket over her chair. As she did so, she leaned forward. Her blouse was partially unbuttoned and I couldn't help but glance down at her chest. I don't know whether her move was intentional. But I must tell you gentlemen. She was a fully developed woman. As much as I take pride in the uniform, it doesn't do justice to a woman like her. And she also smelled of some exotic fragrance. I went literally wild trying to constrain myself."

"Did you make any advances toward her?" Torre asked.

"Heavens no, sergeant. I was in complete control. I must admit, though, that I haven't felt that way in many, many years. My wife and I have had a wonderful relationship since that incident with Leo's wife many years ago. The scars have healed. But I cannot recall the last time I reacted so physically to any woman, including my wife. I struggled but maintained my composure. All I did was sit behind my desk trying not to look obvious. When Jennifer invited me to her apartment for dinner, I reacted spontaneously. I ignored constraint and common sense and agreed to meet her the following Thursday.

I asked what excuse he gave his wife.

"That I had a late meeting and would stay overnight in the city."

"Is that when Jennifer told you about Leo Brandwyne?"

"Not immediately. When I arrived at her apartment, she served me a light meal. She even had my favorite pipe tobacco. After dinner she told me to relax on the sofa while she did the dishes. Later it happened. She came over and sat next to me on the sofa, messing up my hair. For an old geezer like me it was invigorating. I felt as if I was a twenty-year-old man. She must have sensed my physical reaction. The next thing I remember sitting in her bed and her telling me about Ms Konowitz."

"What did she say?"

"She told me that after I asked her to help Leo's kid, she called Ms Konowitz. She asked her to meet the ranger on Liberty Island. She even gave Ms Konowitz a complimentary pass for the ferry. I thought that was funny."

Belmont was more relaxed than when we arrived.

"Jennifer arranged to sneak Ms Konowitz into the monument through a side door that is used only by staff. Ms Konowitz was to wait there. She was to bring Leo's son there a few hours later. Since there are no security cameras in that part of the monument, Ms Konowitz was able to avoid detection. This seemed preposterous but apparently it worked. Leo Junior arrived on schedule and met Ms Konowotz. Jennifer said, however, that he was in a rotten mood. He began to yell and scream that he was being played for a fool and that his father and I were involved in this scheme. He accused Ms Konowitz of being a slut and Jennifer of being party to a scheme to humiliate him. He continued to yell and Jennifer tried to calm him down. When she was not successful, Ms Konowitz told her to leave. She would handle him her way and not to worry. Jennifer reluctantly left the two and reported for duty. When Brandwyne came to the office, Jennifer asked him how things went and he said it was fine. Jennifer didn't know Brandwyne murdered her friend until she found the body the next morning."

"She didn't think that Brandwyne was acting strange?"

"No. He didn't act any differently than he did any other evening. No one suspected a thing," Belmont responded.

Torre and I were speechless.

"Assuming what you told us is true, Sam. How do you account for the fact that William Johnson deviated from routine and didn't open the monument the following morning?" I asked. Although I had defended the deputy chief ranger from the start of the investigation, I was beginning to have my doubts about his innocence.

"I can't answer that. To the best of my knowledge, gentlemen, it was a coincidence. I doubt that Will would be involved. But I have been wrong before."

"Any significance to the fact that Johnson asked Ms Marcus to take his place the following morning? Is this, too, a coincidence?"

"I have to assume so, Michael."

"Did Ms Marcus ask where her friend was hiding?"

"The kid told her she was in the hatchway and that she would be safe. She was comfortable. He said he would volunteer to take the later patrol shifts, claiming he had a headache and wanted the fresh air. He told Varga at around eleven forty-five, in fact, that he needed some exercise and would handle the midnight tour."

"Are you certain Ms Marcus was unaware that her friend was dead?"

"I believe that is a fair statement, lieutenant," the superintendent responded.

"Do you think that Leo discussed this with his father?"

"Unlikely. Leo Senior is a dangerous man. He would do anything to get his way. But I would doubt that he would condone or propose murder. He does have some deep-rooted moral convictions. Murder doesn't fit into that scheme. In answer to your last question, unlikely."

"Have you spoken to Leo Brandwyne's father since then?" I asked.

"I called after the murder. That was the last time we spoke."

"What did you tell him?"

"I said I tried to fix his son with a date and explained the circumstances. He said he was appreciative. He knew about the murder. Read about it in the local paper out west and saw it on the news. He didn't relate the murder to his son or what I did to try to help him."

"He hasn't called you since?" Torre asked.

"No."

"Who told Leo's son about your intervention?"

"I never told him. I'm sure his father didn't. I don't know."

"Anyone else involved in the scheme?" Torre continued.

"I'm unable to determine."

Belmont stared at us. His cup remained untouched on his desk. He rose and walked to where we were sitting.

"Any other questions, gentlemen? I have several important matters awaiting my attention."

"Let me get this straight, Mr. Belmont," Torre said. The Brandwyne boy killed Ms Konowitz. He didn't tell Jennifer Marcus who found out about it when she happened on the body."

"Correct, sergeant."

"You don't know why he killed her."

"Correct again."

I wasn't finished with my questioning. But I doubted we would get any more answers at this time. We left.

Belmont dialed Leo Brandwyne Sr.

Chapter 32

Ron Gaines left a message for me. We met on a park bench in Battery Park in lower Manhattan.

His sweatshirt had frayed sleeves and there were large holes in the knees of his faded jeans. His sneakers were black with grime. Gaines needed a shave and reeked of alcohol.

"I was in love with Jennifer. She was in love with me."

"Was she good in bed, too?" I asked.

"How do you know?"

"A friend told me," I said.

Gaines stared at me but didn't respond.

"She was great in bed. But emotionally she also was good for me."

I smiled.

"You think I'm a pompous ass. I am. But I want to clear the record. I had nothing to do with Jennifer's suicide. She swore her love for me and said she'd never sleep with another man."

"Did you believe her?" I asked. I didn't tell him about Sam Belmont.

"How many rangers have you slept with?"

"No one else. I swear. I try to distance myself but with Jen there was this chemical reaction. We used to meet in my office on business. Then we'd go into Manhattan for coffee. One day I had a late meeting so she invited me to stay over her apartment."

"How'd you explain it to your wife?"

"I was staying with a friend. I never told her and she never asked. I'm married to a wonderful woman. But with Jennifer it was different. When I'm home it's the same bullshit. How much she paid for the kids' shoes. What the neighbor told her about the couple across the street. How long the lines were at the supermarket and how milk has gone up ten cents a half gallon. Frankly I didn't give a damn. I wish to Hell she would get a job and be more worldly. All she does is gossip with the neighbors and with her parents on the phone. When I want to make love, she's always too tired."

"Does she ever question your absences?"

"No. I told her this investigation requires my attention and she goes for it. She's too trusting. That's another thing. Maybe if she demanded explanations I'd be more responsive. Jennifer was an escape valve. Someone I could relate to professionally and discuss world affairs with."

"Don't forget the sex," I reminded him.

Gaines blushed.

"Do you really want your wife to get a job?"

"It would help. Money's tight. Lorelei told me she goes to her parents for food money a couple of times a month. That bothers me. Maybe if she got a part-time job she'd have less to gossip with her parents. I resent their interference. But they are helping pay the bills."

"Have you suggested it?"

"Yeah. Her excuse is that her mother thinks she should be a stay-at-home mom and be with the kids. Every time I make the suggestion she says her mother feels differently."

"She listens to her mother and not you."

"Yes," Gaines whispered.

"Where's the money go? At your pay grade you earn a decent salary."

"You know how it is. I usually brought food when I visited Jen. And occasionally I play the ponies at OTB."

"How much did you know about her plans for Skip Brandwyne?"

"She mentioned something. A favor for the superintendent. Didn't tell me the details."

"What did you tell her?"

"If I know too much I'll have to stop it. I didn't want to know."

"Did she say how Belmont asked her?"

"No."

"So she acted alone with Sam Belmont's knowledge."

"And I guess with his green light."

"How did Shirley Konowitz die?"

"Somebody screwed up, I guess."

"You didn't answer my question"

"How do you expect me to know? I wasn't there. I told you Jen never gave me the details. All I know is that the woman died. Jennifer found the body. You and that friggin' detective have been on my case since then."

"What else can you tell me?"

"Nothing."

"Why did you call me if you don't have anything to tell me?" I asked.

A ferry captain honked his horn. Gaines glanced over my shoulder, watching it steam away from the dock toward Liberty Island.

"Ask William Johnson."

I sat silently staring at the chief ranger.

"Are you recording this conversation?" Gaines asked.

"Why would I do that?"

"I developed distrust of cops."

I assured him our conversation wasn't taped.

"Will's a sly ex-cokehead. He wanted to get rid of Jennifer because he was jealous. She rebuffed his advances. He heard about Ms Konowitz and sneaked into the monument and tried to attack her. She fought him and he choked her. When he ordered Jen to cover for him that morning, he knew she'd find the body."

When I asked Gaines to back up his allegations, he said Jennifer told him.

"Why are you going against your best buddy?" I asked him.

"I'm clean. I'm tired of your heavy-handed nonsense. You asked me a question. I gave you an answer. You don't believe me, do you?"

"You know damn well I must have proof," I countered.

"I know Will's background. Got shot up in 'Nam. That place was awash with heroin and pot. Cocaine wasn't available. He went from morphine to heroin. Back in the States he became a cokehead. He's done a good job of hiding it. He still shoots up at night."

I tried to reason with Gaines but to no avail. I told him that I needed evidence.

"Show me proof," I demanded.

"I lost my sweetheart. My reputation is ruined. I want to close this so I can get on with my life. Do you understand me?" he shouted. Passers-by stopped and stared at us.

I asked him again who knew of Jennifer Marcus' plans. He responded that the entire night staff was aware of it.

"Including Johnson?"

"Yes."

"Including you?"

"I already told you what I knew."

"I don't believe you but I'll pursue your leads," I told him.

Gaines smiled. He walked toward the subway at Bowling Green Station and disappeared.

I watched the Circle Line ferry steam toward Liberty Island.

Chapter 33

William Johnson was tense. It was the first time I had seen him in a suit and tie. I asked him about Skip Brandwyne's social life.

"That's heavy stuff, Mike. You know I can't tell you much. You're going to have to subpoena me. I refuse to violate regulations and the Privacy Act.

"I'll get a court order if I have to. I'm hoping you'll cooperate," I said. Johnson pondered my request.

"Make my life easy. I'll try not to pry too deeply," I assured the deputy chief ranger.

"OK. What do you want to know? Skip's a good ranger. Very bright. Never saw him after hours."

"There's a report he was going to meet a woman inside the monument the night Ms Konowitz died."

"You're pulling my leg. First time I heard that."

"The word is Jennifer Marcus asked a friend to come to the island to meet him. She felt sorry for him and wanted him to meet a woman. Everyone on the island knew about it. And you're telling me you didn't know," I lied.

"Get out of here."

"Will you take a polygraph?"

"You believe some kind of lunatic with a fantastic imagination and you want *me* to take a lie detector test. You're sure the inmates aren't running the asylum?" Johnson rose to leave.

I ordered him to sit down. He reluctantly returned to his chair.

"Honest Mike. I don't know what's going on. In this country you're supposed to be innocent until proven guilty. Now you got some report and you want me to take a lie detector test. I'm thoroughly confused. I'll take the test. I've got nothing to hide."

I believed him despite the many coincidences and allegations.

I asked Johnson about his Vietnam experiences. He reluctantly played down his heroism. He admitted, however, that he was hospitalized for drug addiction.

"I'd think your being at opposite poles during Vietnam would cause problems for you and Gaines," I said.

"We solved our differences early on. I love the Gaines children. Before the death, Ron and Lori would invite me over often. I haven't been there since the body was found."

I asked how many friends the Gaines have. Johnson said no friends within the Park Service. Beyond that he did not know.

"If that woman was on the island to meet Brandwyne, do you think Gaines knew about it?"

"If a ranger set it up, I doubt it. The only thing they would tell Ron was the time. I would doubt even that much."

"Suppose the ranger was Jennifer Marcus?"

Johnson pondered a response.

"I'd assume she told him. He was at her apartment a lot. They must have discussed park issues."

"Did you and Gaines ever discuss Miss Marcus?"

"What do you mean? We're always going over evaluation reports and daily activity sheets."

"Did he ever mention leaving his wife for Ms Marcus?"

"No. That's the God's honest truth. Never said a word."

Johnson hesitated.

"I've got a question for you, Mike. Did my buddy tell you I was involved in the murder?"

I rose from behind my desk. I shook Johnson's hand and opened the door.

Chapter 34

I made an appointment to see a well-known gastroenterologist at the NYU Medical Center in Manhattan. I wanted information on Brandwyne's food sensitivity. The physician handed me a large envelope with brochures and copies of articles that had been published in medical journals. He confirmed that there are varying degrees of sensitivity. Some patients, he said, are more prone to reactions to wheat, rye, oats and barley than others.

"Even a crumb can affect some patients. Others can eat an occasional sandwich with no outward effects. I tell patients to avoid it at all costs," he said.

"Are they able to eat out?" I asked.

"Assuming they alert the waiter and the kitchen is willing to clean the grille."

"In other words, doctor, if a celiac uses his disease as an excuse to avoid eating out, the problem is a cop-out or may be emotional rather than physical."

"I wouldn't go that far. There is plenty to eat. Many restaurants are accommodating. Others can't be bothered. Some celiacs, however, remain fearful of taking the risk. One cannot and should not make a blanket statement about the emotional and physical consequences of this disease," he said.

I had what I was looking for. Now I had to determine the severity of Brandwyne's condition.

Chapter 35

The young ranger was tense and uncomfortable as we sat in a private office on Ellis Island, a short boat ride from the Statue of Liberty. I told him about my conversation with a physician about his disease and asked Skip about his sensitivity to gluten. He said he didn't know the degree of his sensitivity but purposely avoided any possible contact, fearful of the consequences.

"I really don't eat out much. I don't earn much as a ranger and I'm afraid I'll get sick in a public place."

"Accidents will happen," I responded.

He nodded.

"Speaking of accidents, Tell me. What were you doing the night of the murder? Do you think it could have been an accident?"

Brandwyne looked at his hands and began to shift restlessly. His posture tightened suddenly.

"I told you once before. We rotate at the desk, catch up on paperwork and patrol the island and monument. I don't recall what my patrol shift was. It took place a long time ago. I'm sure the duty log has that information. What are you thinking?"

"When you entered the monument. You're sure you saw no one inside?"

Brandwyne looked down at his hands again. He folded and unfolded them and crossed and uncrossed his legs. He seemed ready to implode.

"It was an accident. I swear to you," he said softly, deflating visibly. "I didn't mean to hurt anyone. It was an accident."

"What are you talking about, Skip?" I sat next to the ranger. My arm gently rested on his shoulder. Brandwyne sobbed.

"I was pissed. Remember the first interview? I said that wives are lonely when their husbands are on detail and that sometimes extra-marital relations occur? I was talking about Sam Belmont and my mom. I knew he raped her when my dad was detailed out of the park. She may have enticed Belmont. But that was no excuse for screwing her. Would you believe I've carried that grudge all these years? What really bothered me was that a lot of people knew about the assault and about my mom's drinking. I was embarrassed and humiliated."

Brandwyne stood and walked around the room, his hands clutched behind his back.

"I wanted to come here. I wanted to get even with the superintendent. I figured if I was close to him, I could figure out how to screw the bastard, even if I had to kill someone and plant the body on *his* island. Then, when he arranged through Jennifer for me to meet that young woman he was playing right into my hands. I got a double whammy, didn't I?"

"What do you mean?" I asked.

I also got that bastard Ron Gaines. I guess his career is over, too. That's a crying shame, isn't it? He's too young to retire. I guess he'll find something to do. But without his badge and pistol and authority his life won't be worth very much will it?" Brandwyne smirked.

"Did you really intend to kill Miss Konowitz?"

"When I found out my father called Sam I figured he threatened him. He's got a longer memory than I do. Yes. I really did intend to kill the young woman. It's a shame she had to die that way. But how else could I get even with Belmont for raping my mom?"

"How did you find out your father called Sam Belmont?"

Brandwyne hesitated. He stared at the floor.

"My mother told me. She wrote me a letter. She never got involved. Dad does what he wants to do. He never listens to my mother or asks her advice. She's gone along with him since they were married. She's afraid of him. He can be intimidating when he sets his mind to something and somebody gets in his way."

"Even to your mother?"

"She's no exception. I remember when I was a kid. She'd run to the bedroom and slam the door many times after arguing with my old man."

"Did he ever hit her?"

"Not that I can recall. But sometimes verbal abuse can be more painful."

"Why do you think she called you?"

"She wrote me a letter. She explained that dad felt it was time to call in a chit. He resented my wanting to break the family chain in the park service. I thought he was kidding but he wasn't. He was damned serious. He wasn't going to let me leave."

"So what did you do?"

"When Jennifer told me about wanting to introduce me to a woman, I figured my old man was behind it; that he got Belmont to get her to do it. So I went along with it. I agreed to meet them in the monument. I didn't know how Jen would hide Shirley. Frankly, I didn't give a damn. By the time I got there my anger had reached a fevered pitch. I was fuming. I was mad at the world. I was mad at my father for instigating this by undoubtedly threatening to expose Belmont. I knew that Jennifer was an innocent victim. That added to my hatred of the superintendent, that spineless twerp. I couldn't help myself. I let out my frustrations on Jen. That's when Shirley told her to leave. I guess I was feeling sorry for myself, too."

"How did the murder occur?"

"To tell you the truth, it really was an accident. It didn't turn out the way I had planned it, lieutenant. After Jennifer left the monument it was just the two of us. Miss Konowitz asked where we could go since it was cold and damp where we were standing. I saw that she was getting the chills and was shivering. Seeing her standing there scared and cold softened me. I actually felt sorry for her. I changed my mind. It made me feel good for once in my life, knowing that I could do something to help someone else. But I felt powerful that I held her life in my hands. It was one of the most wonderful experiences I could ask for. I led her to the second floor away from the cameras so that we wouldn't be detected."

"What did you do then?"

"I figured we needed to find a place where we could talk. I knew that the only place where there were no cameras was in the rest rooms so we went into the ladies room. She came over to me and began to hug me. I think she was frightened. That's my guess. Her hands crept up under my shirt and she scratched my back. She thanked me for finding a warm spot where we could chat. She then told me to relax and leave everything to her; everything would be fine, and to trust her. She said she wanted to show me a good time. Shirley then let go and walked into a stall. I could hear her moving around but I didn't know what she was doing. When she came out, she began to unbutton her blouse. When it was completely open I noticed she wasn't wearing anything underneath. She spread the top of her blouse and asked me if I had ever seen breasts like hers. I got carried away. We made love on the bathroom floor."

I didn't believe what I had heard.

"It was wild, lieutenant. I never dreamed sex could be so great. When we were finished, she told me to wait outside the bathroom while she got dressed. That's when I decided to hide her in the hatchway leading to the torch. I told her I'd come back for her in a few hours."

Brandwyne again paced the room.

"About eleven forty-five I signed out. I said I'd check the monument and didn't need any help. I think I said I needed some fresh air and the exercise would be good for me. When I opened the hatchway door she was mad. She fell to the carpet and said she was hot and tired and she had a leg cramp. Miss Konowitz then argued with me that this was no way to treat a lady who had given him the best ride he ever had. She began to hit me and I tried to stop her. I got pissed off again and I strangled her. Who did she think she was talking to and hitting? I wasn't going to take that shit from a two-bit whore. When she fell to the floor I panicked. I wasn't certain anyone saw me in the monitors. I tugged the body out of sight and straightened up her blouse. Then I pulled the body back near the stairs and walked downstairs. I checked the bathroom to make sure she had left no evidence. When I was certain it was clean, I left the monument."

"How would you justify having patrolled the monument at close to midnight and not reporting a body?" I asked.

"I don't know. But the question never came up."

"How would you have responded?"

"The body wasn't there when I made my patrol. There would've been no way to prove otherwise."

I asked why Johnson assigned Jennifer Marcus to make the inspection the following day. Brandwyne speculated it was coincidence.

"The island was packed during the weekend and the temperatures were out of sight. I guess he was tired. I don't blame him," Brandwyne said. He appeared relieved that the secret was in the open.

"Do you think Johnson knew about the murder?"

"Can't say. Unlikely, though."

"Why did you go to Johnson's apartment and tell him you overheard Ms Marcus on the phone?"

"I already told you. My mother wrote me that my dad and Belmont were scheming. I also knew that Jennifer visited Belmont's office on her day off. Usually if there's a problem we come to work early or ask for an hour of leave during our normal shift. We go through the chain of command through Johnson and Gaines. You don't ordinarily go to the superintendent."

I listened intently.

"How'd you know she went to Belmont's office?"

"I have ways of finding out. I keep my eyes and ears open. Just say I inherited my father's genes. I'm a survivor."

I said nothing.

"I figured a good way to smoke out Jennifer was to visit Johnson's apartment and plant the seed of doubt. I'm a conniving bastard. I wanted Johnson to know that I was aware of what was happening and I wanted Jennifer to know that I wasn't so naïve as she thought I was. Eventually Johnson would have to report our conversation to you or someone else on the case, so I made up the story about Jennifer's phone call. I was willing to wait for Belmont to hang by his fingernails. Neat, eh?" Brandwyne smiled broadly.

I continued to remain silent.

"Jennifer and Miss Konowitz were a good team," the younger Brandwyne said.

"Had you ever asked Ms Marcus out on a date?" I asked.

"A couple of times. She always had an excuse, that slut. She was a helluva tease. She always wore that sexy perfume. Even at work. And when she talked to you about business. She had those eyes. She was always teasing the guys with her eyes. I'm surprised Gaines was the only one who got her in bed."

I asked Skip Brandwyne to dictate a statement. We taped his confession in the same office. Park Police detectives who were waiting outside, then took him into custody. Brandwyne was charged with negligent homicide. We didn't have enough evidence to hold him on first or second-degree murder. His lawyer, in fact, would build a defense around emotional instability.

Before he was taken away, Brandwyne asked if he could speak with me alone. I nodded to the detectives that it would be OK.

"I've got to hand it to you, Lieutenant Finnegan. I never thought you'd solve my perfect crime. But I'm at peace with myself. My old man won't get his way with my career and Belmont's through. Best of all, I'll never forget Miss Konowitz's body. Whew! It was the first time and probably the last. I'll never forget it. It was the best sex one could ever have." He shook my hand and left the room. He was whistling Dixie as he closed the door behind him.

Chapter 36

Will Johnson answered after the third ring.

"Are you still mad?" I asked.

"I forgot about it. You have a job to do. Don't sweat the small stuff, Mike," He said.

"It's been bothering me. Why did Gaines try to implicate you?"

"I'm not mad at him. I feel sorry for him," Johnson responded.

The deputy chief ranger related how he received a call from Lorelei Gaines' mother. She wanted to know if her son-in-law talked to him about his marriage.

"The call caught me by surprise. I lied that we were so busy with the investigation we didn't have time to talk about anything else. I felt it wasn't my place to say anything. Then she throws this one at me. 'Who is Ronald seeing on the side?' She never called him by his full name before. She asks if the other woman is good looking. I knew she knew. I told her when we work late, Ron stays at a ranger's apartment in Manhattan. I made sure not to say who he was staying with. I guess she found out there's only two women with law enforcement commissions. She calls Jennifer. She admits she's in love with Gaines."

"You know this for a fact?"

"Jennifer came to my office for a private meeting. You know, like she used to do with Ron. She tells me about the phone call. She cried that Lorelei's mother threatened to sue her for breaking up her daughter's marriage. Lorelei's mom also threatened to investigate to see if criminal charges could be brought against her."

"That still doesn't explain why Gaines would rat on you," I said.

"He thinks I told his mother-in-law. He wasn't convinced that Jennifer would."

"I'm still trying to figure out why you ordered Jennifer Marcus to make the final inspection that morning," I interjected.

"Mike. I'm sounding like a broken record. I was dragging from the weekend. I needed the extra half hour sleep."

Chapter 37

The regional director called Sam Belmont at home. He demanded the superintendent's resignation faxed to the regional office by ten o'clock the following morning. He directed Sam to clean out his desk and be off the island by five o'clock that afternoon. The regional office also requested that no criminal charges be filed. He didn't want any further embarrassment done to the Park Service. A federal prosecutor over-ruled the director, however. Because he resigned, Belmont avoided administrative charges. He could have faced additional penalties resulting from his intimate relationship with Jennifer Marcus.

Prosecutors later charged Belmont with failure to report a crime and improperly administering his office. A federal district court judge in Manhattan imposed a $500 fine and sentenced the former superintendent to three years in prison, suspended after three months, and the remaining time on probation.

Leo Brandwyne Jr. was charged with assaulting a federal officer, Jennifer Marcus, and with involuntary manslaughter. The same federal district judge sentenced him to three years in prison on each count, to run concurrently.

Leo Brandwyne Sr. was found guilty of intimidating a government official and was sentenced to two years in a federal penitentiary.

The rangers on duty all were transferred to other parks within the region. Everyone except Phil Varga, however. I urged the regional director to seek re-assignment for him to New Mexico. The RD complied.

Shortly after Lorelei Gaines was granted a divorce, her ex-husband was admitted to a psychiatric facility for treatment of a nervous breakdown. The regional director appointed Will Johnson to replace him as chief ranger on Liberty Island.

CHAPTER 38

I received a telephone call several months after the death and suicide from Will Johnson.

"Got the polygraph ready? I'm on my way over."

"What are you talking about?" I asked.

"You wanted me to take a lie detector test during the investigation. Don't you remember?"

"Yeah. But Brandwyne is in jail. The case is closed."

"Remember when I went to church for guidance before telling you about Skip Brandwyne's visit? I met a wonderful woman there. The choir director. I asked her last night to marry me and she said yes."

Before I could congratulate him, Will said he had a favor to ask.

"Will you be my best man?"

"But what about the polygraph?"

"I promised Sylvia I'd love, honor, and obey. I want the lie detector tape as evidence because I'm planning to stay married to her for a long time. I want her to know that my word is bond."

I called Marge to tell her the news.

"Go out and buy a pretty new dress. Don't worry about the price. And go to the travel agent and book a flight to anywhere. We need a second honeymoon. And do me a favor. Call my father. Tell him I'll be there in an hour to personally thank him. Say there's no hard feelings. Tell him to get the ice because I'm bringing over a bottle of his favorite scotch."

The End

Printed in the United States
55712LVS00007B/124-129